I'm the
**STRONGEST**
in **ZOMBIE**
This
**WORLD**, but I
Can't
**Beat This Girl!**

**1**

Ryou Iwanami

Illustration by TwinBox

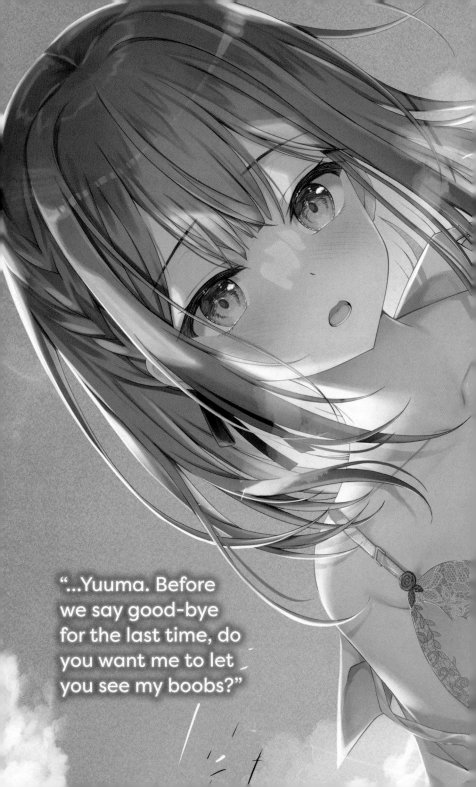

"...Yuuma. Before we say good-bye for the last time, do you want me to let you see my boobs?"

What's going on?
Is this heaven?
Did I die?
Well, I guess I pretty
much did, since I turned
into a zombie...

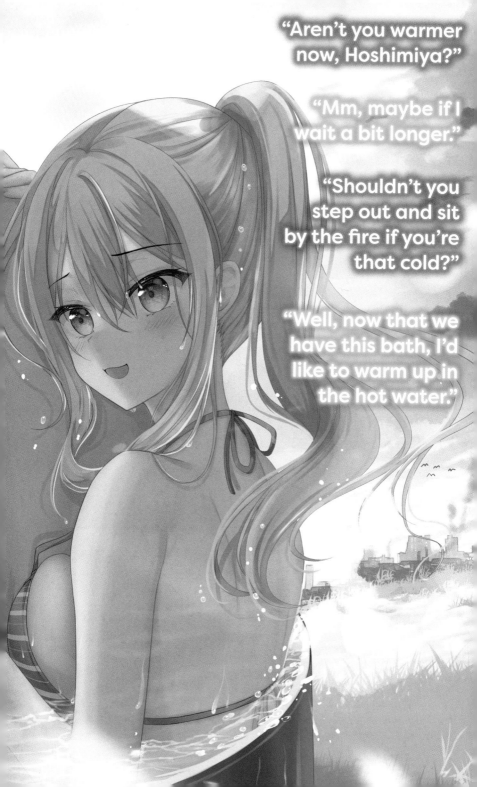

"Aren't you warmer now, Hoshimiya?"

"Mm, maybe if I wait a bit longer."

"Shouldn't you step out and sit by the fire if you're that cold?"

"Well, now that we have this bath, I'd like to warm up in the hot water."

"...Mmm...! ...Aaahh...!"

Our breathing came heavy as
we continued to kiss deeply.
After a while, her hand started
to warm up.

"H...hey, what
are you doing,
cheating on
me in broad
daylight?!"

# CONTENTS

I'M THE STRONGEST IN THIS ZOMBIE
WORLD, BUT I CAN'T BEAT THIS GIRL!

# I'm the STRONGEST in This ZOMBIE WORLD, but I Can't Beat This Girl!

## 1

**Ryou Iwanami**

Illustration by **TwinBox**

YEN ON
NEW YORK

# I'm the STRONGEST in This ZOMBIE WORLD, but I Can't Beat This Girl!

**Ryou Iwanami**

Translation by Eriko Sugita
Cover art by TwinBox

ZOMBIESEKAI DE ORE WA SAIKYODAKEDO, KONOKONIWA KATENAI Vol. 1
© Ryou Iwanami 2023
First published in Japan in 2023 by KADOKAWA CORPORATION, Tokyo.
English translation rights arranged with KADOKAWA CORPORATION, Tokyo through TUTTLE-MORI AGENCY, INC., Tokyo.

English translation © 2024 by Yen Press, LLC

Yen On
150 West 30th Street, 19th Floor
New York, NY 10001

Visit us at yenpress.com ♥ facebook.com/yenpress ♥ twitter.com/yenpress
yenpress.tumblr.com ♥ instagram.com/yenpress

First Yen On Edition: December 2024
Edited by Yen On Editorial: Christopher Fox, Anna Powers
Designed by Yen Press Design: Liz Parlett

Yen On is an imprint of Yen Press, LLC.
The Yen On name and logo are trademarks of Yen Press, LLC.

Library of Congress Cataloging-in-Publication Data
Names: Iwanami, Ryou, author. | TwinBox (Illustrator), illustrator. | Sugita, Eriko, translator.
Title: I'm the strongest in this zombie world, but I can't beat this girl!
 / Ryou Iwanami ; illustration by TwinBox ; translation by Eriko Sugita.
Other titles: Zombie sekai de ore wa saikyou dakedo, kono ko ni wa katenai.
 English | I am the strongest in this zombie world, but I cannot beat this girl!
Description: First Yen On edition. | New York, NY : Yen On, 2024-
Identifiers: LCCN 2024038437 | ISBN 9781975394271 (v. 1 ; trade paperback)
 | ISBN 9781975394288 (v. 1 ; ebook) | ISBN 9781975394295 (v. 2 ; trade paperback)
Subjects: LCGFT: Zombie fiction. | Romance fiction. | Humorous fiction. | Light novels.
Classification: LCC PL879.4.W36 Z6613 2024 | DDC
 895.63/6--dc23/eng/20240820
LC record available at https://lccn.loc.gov/2024038437

ISBNs: 978-1-9753-9427-1 (paperback)
 978-1-9753-9428-8 (ebook)

10 9 8 7 6 5 4 3 2 1

LSC-C

Printed in the United States of America

It was a beautiful sunny day in September, and summer was almost at an end.

The sky was bright and clear as I looked out the window of my third-floor classroom, ignoring whatever it was my math teacher seemed to be saying. I had a feeling something good was going to happen today.

Suddenly, I heard a student yelling in the schoolyard—a low roar that seemed to reverberate all the way to the bottom of my stomach. It was an incredibly urgent sound, but I figured some kids must just be fooling around during PE. Our class was interrupted for a few seconds, but it didn't seem like anything to seriously worry about.

However, the number of voices echoing through the halls kept increasing. A few people naturally became suspicious and went to the balcony to see what was going on—and they screamed.

That drew everyone's attention, so the rest of the class also went out onto the balcony. I followed them and looked below...

Puddles of blood stained the white sand, while several boys in sweats lay collapsed on the ground. I shivered, realizing that the screams I'd heard were cries of terror, and my hair stood on end.

"Someone dangerous might have broken in," the teacher said. "Don't go outside." Then he rushed out of the classroom and ran down the stairs to the first floor.

We looked around the schoolyard in horror. It was then that some of the students lying on the ground rose and began walking unsteadily toward the school building.

"Oh good, they're okay."

"They can't be; look at how much they've bled out."

"Maybe it's a prank."

"A bit much for a prank, don't you think?"

"Could it be for a movie or something?"

We came up with all sorts of different explanations, and the class agreed to wait for our math teacher to return.

Then one of my classmates said a news site he was watching had gone haywire. I checked my phone and saw the word *zombie* splashed across all the headlines, with stories saying an unprecedented disaster was currently taking place throughout the country.

Although we were skeptical, several students tried to call the police, but no one could get through.

It was hell from there on out. Some people panicked and screamed and cried, while others tried desperately to get their hands on anything that might serve as a weapon. The same classmates who'd been laughing with each other only moments earlier began arguing, and I noticed several zombies standing behind the window that looked out into the hallway.

Their skin was gray, and their eyes a cloudy white that made it hard to tell what they were looking at. Saliva dripped from their half-open mouths.

Those unmistakably unearthly monsters swarmed around the door, trying to enter the classroom.

My classmates scrambled out onto the balcony. I tried to follow them, but it was already overflowing with people. The other classrooms were all the same—students panicking and rushing to the balcony with nowhere else to run.

Soon after, the door to our classroom broke down, and the zombies rushed in. Some of my classmates ran out into the hallway, looking for a way out, and I decided to follow them.

The school building was already full of zombies. As classmates running nearby were caught and eaten one after another, I single-mindedly raced down the stairs.

My lungs felt like they would burst, but I knew I would die if I stopped.

In the end, I was the only one who made it off the school grounds.

But outside the school was hell, too. Traffic accidents and fires had broken out everywhere, and black smoke filled the air.

*What the hell's going on...?* The only thing I could think of was that I was asleep and having some sort of terrible nightmare...

The shock of it all was too much, and I couldn't remain standing any longer. I collapsed into a nearby bush and tried to calmly recall what had happened in the past few minutes, but none of it seemed real.

I lay there in a daze for a while, but nothing changed, no matter how much time passed. I didn't seem to be waking up, and there was no sign of anyone else escaping from the school building.

Whatever—I couldn't stay in this spot forever. First, I tried to call my grandparents at home, but I soon realized my phone didn't have reception. Maybe everyone had tried to call to see if their friends were okay, and the server had gone down…

I felt like smashing my phone on the ground, but I managed to control myself. Maybe I'd get a signal later.

Still, I had no way to call for help. I had to do something on my own…

I made up my mind. I started walking home.

I couldn't use the train, though, of course, and I came across a lot of zombies on the road. I managed to get away since they moved so slowly, but I was getting exhausted, and it ended up taking me more than five hours to get home.

Barely making it back alive, I finally stepped inside my house and heard the sound of the TV coming from the living room. I spotted Mom's shoes in the entryway and figured she must have come home from work.

I locked the door so zombies couldn't come in, then went into the living room, where I saw my mom, grandmother, and grandfather all standing there with their backs to me. I called out to them.

The three of them staggered and turned around: They were all zombies.

Their eyes were clouded, and their mouths hung slack. They were no longer the people I'd once known.

Standing there motionlessly, my brain no longer functioning, they must have seen me as prey. Those things that had previously been my family were now coming to eat me.

I quickly regained my senses and ran, but in the time it took me to unlock the front door, one of them bit my right hand.

I shook off my attacker and ran outside, charging ahead without looking back.

The thought crossed my mind that maybe it was only a shallow bite, and I'd be safe, but I was too scared to look at the wound.

# DAY 1

A wind blew across the houses, coated with the smell of blood.

No more screams pierced the air. All I could hear were the moaning cries of zombies.

I fearfully looked at the wound on my right hand; the base of my little finger had been bitten, and the area around it had turned gray. I couldn't bend my pinkie or ring finger properly anymore, either.

My entire body was filled with fatigue, and with every passing second, I felt closer to death. Soon, I would just become another hideous monster roaming around in search of prey...

Overcome with despair, I stepped out onto the main road. The zombies all around me immediately turned and looked toward me, but they lost interest when I raised my graying right hand. I guess they didn't attack people who were already on their way to becoming zombies.

*So I can freely roam this world?* I laughed at myself for having a thought like that. It was the most meaningless discovery I'd ever made.

Aimlessly wandering down the road, I eventually came to a

riverside where I'd often played as a child. There were no zombies around.

I fell onto the weed-covered slope and gazed out at the stagnant river before me. *This is the last sight I'll ever see...*

It had been a while since I was bitten, so it was probably going to happen anytime now. I had to prepare myself.

—*No. I don't want to die.*

To hell with that. I didn't want to cease to exist as myself.

What would happen to my consciousness after I died? The more I thought about it, the more scared I became...

I was devastated, imagining the future that would become my reality in only a few minutes, when I heard footsteps approaching. I'd gotten so used to seeing zombies by that point, I didn't even bother to check who it was.

*Go ahead and bite me if you want to eat me—*

"...Yuuma Kousaka...? Is that you...?"

As I sat there drowning in a sea of despair, a beautiful, clear voice called out my name. Stunned, I looked up and saw a girl with black hair standing in front of me, wearing the uniform of an all-girls high school.

"Yeah..."

"Thank goodness...!! You're alive...!!"

She smiled with relief, tearing up a bit. The scenery had seemed gray only a moment ago, but now it turned to color where she stood.

"...Uh, who're you?"

"Haruka Hyuuga!"

"Haruka Hyuuga... Takuya's younger sister?"

"Yes!"

Hyuuga wiped a tear from her eye and smiled as brightly as a cloudless sky. Seeing her like that, I couldn't help but smile, too.

Who would've thought I'd run into the sister of one of my elementary school friends during the final moments of my life?

"Wow, I haven't seen you in ages. It's been what, five years? How'd you recognize me?"

"You used to come over practically every day. I'm more surprised that you'd forgotten me."

"We were still in grade school back then. You're in your first year of high school now? Wow, you look so different."

"Hee-hee. Thanks."

Hyuuga smiled and began walking toward me.

I suddenly regained my senses.

"—Stop! Don't come near me!"

"Huh...? What's wrong...?"

"...I was bitten by a zombie..."

"—?!"

Hyuuga was speechless, her eyes wide.

"N-no..."

"That's why it's dangerous for you to get too close. You have to get away from here right now."

"...I don't want to do that," she said, lowering herself to sit next to me. I reflexively jumped back.

"Hey! I told you not to get any closer!"

It was only after I'd shouted at her that I noticed tears welling up in Hyuuga's eyes.

"I want to talk to you some more... So please, let me stay with you until you're not human anymore..." Tears were running down her face.

"Aren't you scared? I could turn into a zombie at any moment..."

"...Aren't *you* scared of going through it alone?"

The words got stuck in my throat. I'd be lying if I'd told her I wasn't afraid.

"I can't do anything to help," she said, "but at least let me sit next to you until you die."

I almost cried with her, hearing those words.

There was no way I could let her do something so dangerous. I had to get away from Hyuuga right now. Even though I knew that, I couldn't help but think how grateful I'd be to have her here by my side.

I couldn't think of anything that would make me happier than to take her up on that.

"...No," I said. "I appreciate the offer, but it's too dangerous."

"Oh wait, that came out wrong... It sounded like I was the one doing you a favor, but I'd say it's more than ninety percent for me. I'm just so exhausted; I don't know how much longer I can keep going..."

I could tell everything from the way she'd said that.

"Hyuuga, were there zombies at your school, too?"

"Yes... All my friends were bitten... I was the only person able to escape, but when I went to see what was going on at home, no one was there... My phone doesn't have a signal, either..."

"Ah..."

I knew how she felt, so badly it hurt. It's impossible to describe that feeling of loss when the world around you suddenly falls apart and you lose everything. It shouldn't be a surprise if she'd lost the will to go on.

"I was plodding along, not knowing what to do, when there you were. I wanted someone to talk to, so I'm really glad I found you."

"Hyuuga, don't tell me you're thinking of having me bite you when I turn into a zombie?"

"Don't worry; I'm not that desperate… But it would be nice if you let me rest with you a little while longer."

"…All right. You can be with me when my life comes to an end," I told her and sat down again in the same spot I'd been in before.

Hyuuga was going to have to live alone in this harsh world; the least I could do was talk to her and help her calm down.

She sat right next to me and looked into my face.

In that moment, a memory of the two of us spending time together on this riverbank flashed through my mind.

"…Now that I think about it, you used to be pretty stubborn. You never listened to me once you'd made up your mind."

"Oh! So you do remember me?"

"Yeah. I was thinking about how I often used to bump into you around here after you'd had a fight with Takuya and run away from home."

"Oh yeah, I remember. You were always the one who found me when I was waiting here by the river."

"This spot is halfway between our homes, so I was sure to pass by."

"I'd always come here when I wanted you to listen to my complaints."

"You did? I thought it was just a coincidence…"

"All those times? Of course it wasn't a coincidence. I pretended to run away from home and came here to wait for you." Hyuuga smiled shyly. "By the way, do you remember the first time we met?"

"Oh yeah. Your brother and I were playing a racing game with friends, and you barged in, saying you wanted to play, too. Five of us were playing a four-player game, so we said the loser had to sit out every round… But you never gave up the controller."

"That's right. My brother got really mad at me, but you played peacemaker and took my place when I lost a round."

"And after that, you came to me whenever you had a problem. Like when you spilled orange juice on Takuya's manga."

"Oh, I remember that! We couldn't figure out how to fix it, though, so we decided to bury it in the backyard instead to hide the evidence."

"Y'know, come to think of it, we could've just put it in a trash for the garbage collectors to pick up."

"Yeah, definitely. Still, I have fond memories of you appointing me to stand guard while you dug a hole in the ground. I was so nervous the whole time."

"Is it still buried in your backyard?"

"Probably. I'll dig it up when I get home."

"It's like a time capsule."

"I didn't want to go home to an empty house, but now I'm feeling a little less scared."

"I'm sure your family's safe and sound. Don't worry about me; go home and do whatever you can to make it through this. The moment our conversation's over, assume I've turned into a zombie and run for your life."

"You're so nice, worrying about me at a time like this... In that case, we'll have to keep talking so I can tell when you become a zombie. This is a big responsibility for me, since it's going to be the last conversation you'll ever have as a human being."

Hyuuga took my hands and squeezed them.

I couldn't help smiling, seeing her like that. Hyuuga was trying to do everything she could for me, and I was overwhelmed by her kindness. Who would've thought my heart would feel so warm in the face of death?

Just being with Hyuuga filled me with hope.

At the same time, it felt so painful; the more we talked, the more I didn't want to die.

I didn't let her see that, though, of course, and continued talking as calmly as I could.

"Now that you've said this is gonna be the last conversation of my life, I have no idea what to talk about."

"Then I'll give you random prompts. How have you been these past five years without seeing me?"

"It's hard to sum up five years in a few words… But I guess it has been pretty normal. There were some fun times—and some tough times as well."

"Uh-huh, I see… So did you find yourself a girlfriend?"

"Sadly not."

"Oh reeeally?"

"Don't laugh."

"I'm not laughing. Hee-hee-hee."

"That's the biggest smile I've seen on your face all day."

"You're just imagining it… Don't keep staring at me."

Hyuuga covered her mouth with both hands, but I could see the corners of her eyes crinkle with glee.

"Is it really that funny to hear about someone being unhappy?"

"It's not that. Besides, not having a girlfriend doesn't necessarily mean you're unhappy."

"Maybe you're right… But when you reach the end of life like this, you start to regret all the things you never did…"

"I see… Then I'll take care of that for you. From now on, I'll be your girlfriend."

"Huh…?!"

"Hey, why are you suddenly speechless?"

"I mean, I just never expected you to suggest that."

"…Don't you want me to be your girlfriend…?"

Hyuuga started to tear up, and I rushed to reassure her. "I didn't say that… Even if I'm on the verge of death, it makes me really happy to have a girlfriend."

"O-oh…okay. Hee-hee-hee…"

Hyuuga hunched her shoulders and smiled shyly.

I was honestly happy to have a cute girl like her as my girlfriend, even if it was only in my dying moments.

"…Um, so okay, we're dating. How about holding hands?"

"No, that's dangerous. I might turn into a zombie and grab you, and you might not be able to get away."

"Just for a little while, then." As soon as the words left her lips, she put her left hand on top of my right.

Her eyes instantly widened in surprise.

"Your hands are freezing!"

"Well, I *am* turning into a zombie. My body temperature must be dropping."

"O-okay… So you must be really close…"

"It must feel creepy, like you're touching a corpse, right? You don't have to force yourself to hold my hand."

"It's not creepy at all," Hyuuga said firmly, wrapping my hand in both of hers. "I'll do my best to warm you up."

My hand had already started to lose feeling, but I could still feel her gentle warmth flowing into me.

I'd never held hands with a girl before. So this was what it was like…

For a moment, I forgot all about the reality of my situation and was genuinely smitten.

"…Thanks. I'm really happy right now."

"Hee-hee-hee. I'm so glad... By the way, is there anything else you want to do with your girlfriend? ...I'll do anything I can to help you."

"...You will...?"

I could hear a devil whispering in my ear.

There was only one thing I wanted to do right now.

I wanted to squeeze her boobs.

As memories of five years ago came back to me, I remembered the vague crush I'd had on her at the time.

If I could have my wish, I wouldn't care about dying.

She was bound to despise me if I told her that, though, and the last thing I wanted was to die with Hyuuga hating me.

Then again, I'd regret it for the rest of my life if I didn't. Even if for the rest of my life was only another minute...

I had a serious choice to make: I could either embarrass myself and die with one last incredible memory or tough it out and turn into a zombie with lingering regrets.

That was when I realized that my left hand was also turning gray. I still had feeling in my fingers, but I couldn't move them smoothly.

Death was fast approaching.

Having gone back and forth in my mind, I turned to the girl beside me. "...Hyuuga. I have a favor to ask, and it's the last thing I'll ever ask of you," I said in a feeble voice. "Will you let me touch your breasts, just a little?"

"—Huuuh?!"

Guess she wasn't expecting that. The sound Hyuuga let out was close to a scream.

Then she covered her breasts with her hands and said shyly,

"Don't people generally want to kiss in a situation like this...? Geez, Yuuma, your mind is filled with all sorts of naughty thoughts..."

She looked appalled, the disbelief evident in her eyes.

I don't know what other people usually think of when they're about to die, but I quickly made up an excuse.

"Uh, it's not what you think. Kissing was the first thing that came to mind, of course, but I didn't want to risk infecting you with the zombie virus."

That was all just a big lie: Squeezing her boobs was absolutely the first thing I'd thought of. In fact, kissing hadn't even occurred to me.

"...That makes sense. You're right; a kiss *would be* dangerous..."

Hyuuga seemed convinced. She was so naive.

"That said, it isn't good to let a guy you aren't even in love with touch your breasts. Forget I asked. I'm sorry I made you feel uncomfortable."

I apologetically bowed my head to the girl I'd just started dating.

But when I looked up a few seconds later, our eyes met. Her face was bright red.

"...Just for a few seconds."

"—Huh?"

Hyuuga continued in a whisper. "...If it's just for a few seconds, I give you permission to touch my breasts."

"—?! A-are you sure...?! You aren't put off by a guy like me touching you...?"

"It's okay... I do kind of like you," Hyuuga murmured softly.

She took her hands away from her chest and glared at me.

"...Here. Go ahead."

"I can't do it when you're scowling at me like that..."

"How I look has nothing to do with my boobs."

"That's not really the problem…"

"Hurry up. It's embarrassing having to wait," Hyuuga said with reproach in her voice. The bright-red color of her face had reached her ears now. Maybe she was only glaring at me to hide her own embarrassment.

I lowered my gaze. That swelling unique to women had grown considerably during the few years we hadn't seen each other.

I never imagined something like this happening with a girl I'd once had a crush on…

"…Then here goes…"

I decided to touch them before she changed her mind.

I hesitantly moved my hands closer and closer to her chest, until I was eventually met with a moment of joy. The sensation against my fingertips was bouncy with just the right amount of elasticity.

"Ah…!"

Hyuuga twitched and exhaled seductively.

I wrapped my hands around the two bulges and felt a blissful softness beneath her slightly stiff clothing. I slowly moved my fingers, and the mounds changed shape.

"Ah…! Mm…!"

Sultry noises escaped her lips, and Hyuuga looked at me shyly. Back when we were in grade school, I never would have imagined she could look as sexy as she did right now. Hyuuga had grown from a girl into a woman.

"—Th-that's enough!"

Hyuuga covered her chest with her hands and put a little distance between us. She looked at me embarrassedly.

"…S-so how was it…?"

"How do I describe it…? I won't have any regrets now, no matter when I die…"

"Y-you liked it that much…?" Hyuuga smiled shyly and stared at me again. "You always did love women's breasts, ever since grade school."

"—What?! No way that's true."

"I'm sure of it. I remember one time we were watching a zombie movie at my house, and there was a scene where the actress took a bath and you could see her breasts. Your eyes were glued to the screen the entire time."

"Huh…?! Really? I don't remember that."

"Well, I do. You were so focused on the screen you didn't even notice me watching you. It was appalling to see what guys are capable of."

"Maybe I was just really concentrating on the movie."

"You were grinning like a total lech."

"How do you remember everything so clearly? Why were you watching me instead of the movie?"

"I'd been thinking about how big the actress's boobs were and wanted to see how you reacted to them."

"That's just mean."

"…Back then, I was a little jealous, seeing how you stared at her… But I've grown up now… Almost as much as that actress."

I couldn't help lowering my gaze when she said that.

"…Should I guess what you're thinking now, Yuuma?"

"You don't even have to say it."

"You want to see mine naked, too."

"…You're right, but so what?"

I couldn't help but admit it, and Hyuuga looked at me with an appraising eye.

Her lips trembled as she asked me a question.

"…Yuuma. Before we say good-bye for the last time, do you want me to let you see my boobs?"

"—What?!!"

Hyuuga looked perplexed by my sudden shout, and I hastily added, "A-are you sure you don't mind…?!"

"I *do* sort of mind, but considering the circumstances… Besides, I might get bitten by a zombie and die soon, too… It must be fate that brought us together here, so I figure it might not be a bad idea to make a few last memories of my youth."

"Don't you think this is a bit adult to be called a memory of your youth?"

"You don't want to see my boobs, then?"

"No, I do. Sorry, I just couldn't stop myself from making a joke. Please do me the great honor of allowing me to see your breasts," I said with a deep bow.

Hyuuga took a deep breath. I looked back up to see her standing right in front of me, her eyes cast down as she silently removed her uniform's jacket. Next, she began unbuttoning her shirt, starting from the top, gradually exposing her bare skin, until eventually her shirt was completely open, revealing a cute pink bra.

Hyuuga's face was bright red, and she didn't make eye contact. Her lips were pressed into a thin line, as if to stifle her embarrassment, and she undid the front hook of her bra with a trembling hand.

But that was where she stopped. She seemed to hesitate, as anyone would in this situation.

It didn't take long for her expression to change to one of resolve, however, and she slowly began to remove her bra.

Free at last, her shapely breasts bounced. Everything—the milky white mounds and their peach-colored tips—was in full view.

I was so shocked I thought my brain might boil over. I couldn't think straight anymore.

One thing I did know, though, was that this was no time to turn into a zombie.

"...Okay, that's it."

After about two seconds, Hyuuga closed her shirt, turned around, and began fixing her clothes.

I thought I should say something, but nothing came to mind. My brain was too busy processing what had just happened.

Hyuuga seemed to have finally finished straightening herself up, but she kept standing there with her back turned to me. She must've been feeling pretty uncomfortable.

Standing there, watching her small back—the *change* came over me.

My eyes were open, but it felt as if my vision was gradually narrowing. The next second, I realized I could no longer move my arms. The end had finally come.

*This is bad! Hyuuga's back is still turned to me—*

"...Hyuu...ga..."

I called out to her, but my tongue wouldn't move the way I wanted it to. I couldn't speak properly, as if my entire mouth had been anesthetized.

"…Quick…get awa…"

I somehow managed to squeeze out those few brief words, and Hyuuga slowly turned around.

"Ha-ha… That was a million times more embarrassing than I thought it would be…," she mumbled as she looked at me. Then her eyes went wide.

"…Wow, you look a lot more like a zombie now."

"Ru…run…"

"Sorry, but I'm not running. I'm going to have you bite me and become a zombie."

"Wh…wha…?"

"I'm tired, and I don't want to be alone. I'd rather give in and turn into a zombie than say good-bye to you. Oh, I know! Why don't you infect me with a kiss instead of a bite? It's more romantic that way. Then we can tie our hands together with a piece of string so we'll stay together even after we're both zombies, and neither of us will ever have to be lonely." Hyuuga took my hand, her eyes shining with hope.

She couldn't do that. There's no way you can just give in and let yourself die.

"Yuuma… Good-bye…," Hyuuga mumbled with an expression of resolve. She slowly moved her face closer to mine.

It was all my fault. If I'd been more forceful pushing her away, maybe Hyuuga wouldn't have given up on living…

My vision had turned gray, my consciousness seemed on the verge of fading, and all the joints in my body were as hard as rocks. But I gathered up the last of my strength and forced out a single word from deep inside.

"…D…on't…"

Hearing my raspy voice, Hyuuga stopped moving.

"—Hmm? What did you say?"

"...Don't..."

"Are you trying to tell me not to become a zombie?"

"...Ye...s..."

"There's no point living in a world like this, though. You can't tell me not to become a zombie when it's happening to you. It's irresponsible. If you want me to keep on living, then stay with me forever."

The moment I heard Hyuuga's pained words, I suddenly felt a heat inside my heart. It slowly spread throughout my body, as if it was moving through all my organs. Every cell in my body seemed to be rejecting my fate.

I had to protect Hyuuga. That was my duty.

I gritted my teeth. My arms felt like lead, but I slowly managed to lift them up through sheer determination.

"...I...will stay...with you...!!"

"Wha—?!"

"...I...will protect...you... I swear it!!"

I squeezed out my voice and grabbed her shoulders with both hands.

Only seconds earlier, Hyuuga had looked completely gray, but then she suddenly regained her normal color, and our eyes met.

"...Um, Yuuma? Is it just me, or are you speaking normally again?" she asked, wide-eyed.

Then it hit me: That paralyzed feeling I'd had was gone, and I could move my hands again, though they were still gray. I no longer had chills or felt exhausted. My narrowed vision was back to normal.

"...Guess the zombification stopped."

"It's *stopped*...?" Hyuuga asked with an incredulous look,

staring at my face. "...Um, this seems a bit hard to ask, but are you sure you haven't already become a zombie?"

"—What?"

"Well, your eyes are cloudy, and your skin's gray. Appearance-wise, you really look the part."

"Huh?! I do?"

I immediately pulled out my phone, turned on the camera, and checked my face.

"—?!!"

Hyuuga was right. No matter how I looked at it, I had the face of a zombie.

"...Huh?! What's going on?"

"That's what I should be asking you."

"Maybe...I managed to retain my mind. Did I hang onto my consciousness even as a zombie?"

"Don't ask me."

"Right. What do I do now, though?"

"How should I know? ...I let you see my boobs thinking you were about to die..."

"Oh, uh, well..."

"This wasn't the deal! You better take responsibility!"

Hyuuga covered her breasts with her hands and pressed her face close to mine, tears in her eyes. I couldn't help but avert my gaze.

"Forget what you just saw! Erase it from your memory right now!"

"I don't think that's how it w— Urgh. Aaaaargh!"

"Don't think you can fool me by pretending!"

She'd seen right through me. Even though I looked exactly like a zombie.

"W-wait a minute! I'm sure I'll turn into a zombie on the inside as well any second now!"

Yet ten minutes later, there was still no sign I was losing my self-awareness.

Was it really possible that I might not turn into a zombie completely...?

"This is terrible. Your mind still hasn't been taken over," Hyuuga said with a reproachful glare, her cheeks puffing out in annoyance.

"I never thought this would happen, either, so won't you please just calm down...?"

"No."

"Yeah, didn't think so..."

"Don't get me wrong; I'm happy you haven't lost your consciousness, but I just can't accept this... This black mark on my life will never go away as long as you're alive..."

"Wasn't it supposed to be a memory of your youth?"

"It *would* have become that the moment you died... But I never would've let you see my breasts if I'd known you wouldn't completely turn..."

Hyuuga bit her lip. She seemed to regret her rash behavior under those extreme conditions with every fiber of her being.

"I'm really sorry. I'll do anything if it means you'll forgive me."

"...Anything...?" Hyuuga's eyes glittered suspiciously while she continued to pout. "Do you really mean that?"

"O-of course."

"Then you'll be a dog if I ask you to be one?" she pressed, an overbearing look in her eyes.

"…Naturally."

I hadn't expect her to ask that of me, but I had no other choice but to accept. She seemed satisfied with my response.

"Good. Now, 'shake,'" she said, holding out her left palm.

"……"

Convincing myself that this was just some sort of game to improve her mood, I placed my right hand on her palm.

"Good boy," she said. "This time, try speaking to me before you give me your paw. Ready, 'shake.'"

"…Okay."

"Hmm? You're a dog. Why are you speaking like a human?"

This was really starting to get on my nerves…

"…*Woof.*"

"Aw, how cute! I think I'll take a video."

"Uh, I don't think that's a good idea…"

"Yuuma. What words can a dog use?"

"…*Hrrn.*"

"I don't understand what you're saying, but a dog would never complain about me taking a video," she said pulling out her phone and aiming the camera at me.

Hyuuga offered her palm again.

"One more time. 'Shake.'"

"……"

I guess I didn't really have the right to refuse. Hyuuga had let me see her breasts to make me happy, so something like this was the least I could do…

Since there was no longer any risk of the video being spread all over the internet, I decided to go along with it.

"*Woof.*"

"Well done! Next, 'sit.'"

"...*Woof.*"

"Great job! What a good doggy I have."

Hyuuga looked down at me with a satisfied smile and put her phone back in her pocket.

"Aren't you hungry, by the way?"

"*Woof.*"

"Hey, I asked you that as a human, so you should answer like you normally would. You should've been able to figure that out if you'd thought about it a little."

"This is ridiculous..."

"What was that?"

"Nothing."

I'd let down my guard. Hyuuga still hadn't forgiven me, so I couldn't talk back to her. I stood up from my spot on the ground and asked her a question.

"Are you hungry?"

"Uh-huh. I haven't eaten anything since breakfast."

"Okay. I'll go get us something."

"...You're sure you'll be okay?"

"Yeah. Those zombies didn't attack me after I got bitten, so they must not target each other. Tell me whatever you want to eat, and I'll go get it for us."

"Then...I want sushi. And pudding, cream puffs, and apple juice."

"Hang on a second." I quickly pulled out my phone and started taking notes. I could probably get everything she wanted at a convenience store.

"Okay, I'm off."

But just as I was setting out to leave, Hyuuga suddenly grabbed me by the sleeve.

"—You'll really, truly be okay?"

"...Of course I will. Just trust me and wait right here."

It was dangerous to leave Hyuuga alone, so I quickly headed to a convenience store about five minutes away.

All the zombies I'd encountered so far had moved slowly, but it seemed like the structure of their bodies allowed them to run normally.

After running for a while, I noticed I wasn't feeling any fatigue. My lungs didn't hurt, even when I kept sprinting as fast as I could, and I didn't even seem to need to breathe in the first place. I had to take air into my lungs when I wanted to say something, but other than that, I was fine not breathing.

What was with this body? It was way too accommodating.

As I went from a riverbed up to a four-lane bridge, I saw a few zombies here and there. Since I was also a zombie, I figured I'd have no problem passing them by, but—

"Aaaargh!!"

A male, middle-aged zombie almost bit me on the shoulder as I tried to slip past him, and I reflexively pushed him away with both hands.

I couldn't believe how much power I had; the zombie flew about three meters away. Apparently becoming a zombie had also strengthened my muscles considerably.

The next thing I knew, five zombies standing nearby turned to look at me as one, all baring their teeth. For some reason, they seemed to recognize me as an alien. Was it because I'd retained my consciousness?

Regardless, I had no time to deal with them right now. I had to get back to Hyuuga as quickly as possible, so instead I decided to ignore the zombies attacking me. I slipped past them and dashed into a nearby convenience store. Seven zombies, made up of both customers and clerks, were already inside, and the moment the automatic doors opened, they stared at me. A shiver ran down my spine.

I didn't have time to be scared, though. I grabbed a shopping basket in my left hand, shoved the zombies out of the way, and tossed a pack of sushi and pudding into the basket.

"Graaar!!"

The zombies tried to attack me from all directions. They really were a pain in the neck, getting up and coming back no matter how many times I pushed them away.

Still, I didn't want to hurt them. They might have stopped moving if I'd destroyed their heads like they did in the movies, but I didn't want to do that to something that had been human just a little while ago—

"Raaargh!"

A young clerk-zombie caught me off guard and bit my left arm. It was so repulsive it made all the hair on my body stand on end.

Her eyes looked insane as her teeth remained sunk into my flesh, showing no signs of letting go. I grabbed her lower jaw with my right hand, pried her mouth open, and pushed her away.

It was only after freeing myself that I realized something: It hadn't hurt. It seemed you lost all sense of pain when you became a zombie. I guess that made sense considering the biology of zombies, as pain would only be a hindrance.

Since I was already a zombie, it also didn't matter if one bit me. I checked the bite mark and saw a teeth-shaped tear in my shirt, but no sign of a wound on my arm. It appeared to have already healed.

I really hadn't expected to be able to regenerate. A zombie body was way too overpowered in this world.

Pushing the zombies out of the way, I went around the store gathering items and soon had everything I needed. All the clerks had already been turned into zombies, so I didn't bother paying and just headed back to Hyuuga.

Not wanting the zombies to follow me, I lured them into the back of the store, then grabbed my shopping basket and ran out the front.

After checking to make sure I wasn't being followed, I returned to the riverbank.

Hyuuga was exactly where I'd left her. Thankfully, it didn't seem like she'd been attacked by zombies.

"Yuuma!! You're back!!" she shouted with joy, beaming as she ran toward me. "Are you okay?! I'm sure you must have run into some zombies!!"

"Yeah. The convenience store was full of them, but it was no biggie. Here's the stuff you wanted."

Hyuuga's eyes lit up when I handed her the shopping basket.

"Yuuma, you're amazing! You really are invincible!"

"It was a piece of cake. Let me know if there's ever anything else you want. Anyway, this is everything you asked for, right? I figured it'd be a hassle washing our hands, so I also grabbed some wet wipes."

"That's so thoughtful of you...!! You're incredible!!" Hyuuga looked so impressed as she stared at me with adoration in her eyes.

But the next second, she began turning over the pack of sushi and cream puffs in the basket, searching for something.

"Uh, what about chopsticks? And a spoon to eat the pudding with?"

"—Oops. I forgot."

"That's okay. We can eat sushi with our hands and save the pudding for later."

Hyuuga put the shopping basket on the ground, cleaned her hands with a wet wipe, and opened the sushi pack. Then she looked around.

"Is there someplace to put this...? Yuuma, could you hold out your hands for a minute, palms up?"

"Like this?"

"Try to keep them as flat as you can... Okay, now don't move until I finish eating."

Hyuuga placed the sushi pack in my right hand and its lid in my left, then squeezed the little packet of soy sauce into the lid.

She hadn't told me she'd been planning to use my hands as a makeshift table...

"...Mmm, it's delicious!"

Hyuuga popped a piece of tuna sushi in her mouth, and a brilliant smile filled her face. I didn't mind putting up with some things to see her smile like that.

"Do you want some?"

"Nah, I'm okay. Maybe it's because I'm a zombie, but I don't feel hungry."

"What? Then you aren't going to eat anymore?"

"I guess not... I don't know if my organs are working, either, so who knows what'd happen to any food I did eat..."

"I see..."

"So don't worry about me. Just eat as much as you want."

"Thank you."

Hyuuga must have been starved; she filled her mouth with one piece of sushi after another.

"By the way, aren't you losing your appetite using me, a zombie, as your table?"

"Huh? Why would I?"

"What d'you mean 'why'? Because zombies are gross."

"Hmmm… I don't like zombies who are strangers, but I don't have a problem with you because you're creepy-cute."

"C-creepy-cute?"

"Yeah. I like horror movies, so I have a tolerance for monsters."

Hyuuga looked me up and down as she ate her sushi. It seemed she'd really meant that and hadn't just said it because she was trying to be nice.

Once Hyuuga finished her sushi, she gorged herself on a cream puff and some apple juice.

"Thank you for the food. I never thought I'd be eating sushi in this sort of situation. I'll enjoy the pudding later, when I find a spoon." Sounding content, she put the pudding in a pocket of her school uniform. It must have been because her stomach was full, but she was all smiles.

—Suddenly her expression clouded over.

"What are we going to do now…?"

"Hmmm… Well, we can't stay here forever. It'd be good if there was safe building somewhere…"

"Do you think anyone else is still alive besides us?"

"This area is full of zombies, so if there *are* any survivors, they have to be laying low. In which case, we have no way of finding them."

"And my phone still has no reception… I wonder what's going on with the police and the Self-Defense Forces."

"I passed a police box by the train station on my way back from the convenience store, and the police officers there had all turned into zombies… I wonder what the situation's like with the Self-Defense Forces. Their garrison is pretty far from here, isn't it?"

"Yeah. If this were a zombie movie, you could imagine the Self-Defense Forces flying in to the rescue in a helicopter."

"And we'd signal them with a bonfire or a flare. Maybe we should have something ready to go in case a helicopter does fly by."

"Smoke flares are easy enough to find; they're equipped in every car."

"Oh, okay. Then I can go back home and—"

All of a sudden, a memory of my zombified mom and grand-parents flashed through my mind. If I went home, I'd run into the zombies of the people who'd once been my family. It wouldn't matter if they bit me now, but I didn't want to see them like that again if I could help it.

What had they been doing inside the house? I wished I could give them a proper burial, but there was still the possibility they'd regain consciousness like I had. The only thing I could do was leave them alone for a while and see.

I wanted to know why I was the only person who could stay human. But was there even a way to find out with the world devastated like this…?

"Um… Yuuma? What's the matter?" Hyuuga asked, looking at me with concern.

"Never mind, it's nothing… There's no one at your house, right?"

"Right. And my parents commute by train, so our car is there."

"Then why don't we head to your place? Your family might have come home, too."

"Are you sure? I don't mind going to yours…"

"Uh, that might not be a very good idea."

"Oh? Why is that?"

"It's just… I checked it out not too long ago, and a fire was burning really close by. There's no telling when it might spread to our house."

I lied on the spot; I didn't want to tell Hyuuga my family had become zombies and have her feel sorry for me.

"A fire…? I'm sorry to hear that. And you can't even call the fire department…"

"It was bound to happen at a time like this. Anyway, that's why we should go to your place."

"Okay."

With that settled, we set out for Hyuuga's home.

I couldn't afford to let my guard down even for a second. I had to protect her—

But just then, out of nowhere, zombies started falling from the sky.

Simply put, a zombie is a moving corpse. Its heart has stopped beating, and it has no body heat. From a biological standpoint, it's dead. And yet somehow, zombies are able to move around, defying all logic and common sense.

Watching them, I've come to understand that zombies have no will of their own but simply react on instinct. They move slowly in response to sounds, smells, and other signs of life—and bite down hard with their strong jaws when they spot prey. That much at least is just like the movies.

I don't know why people become zombies when they're bitten, but often in media, their saliva contains a virus that invades a victim's body and transforms them. I'm not sure if that's the case here, though…

How to stop them is also unclear. Film logic says that if you crush their head or decapitate them, a zombie will stop moving. But in the real world…

These were the sorts of thoughts going through my mind when a zombie suddenly fell headfirst onto the ground in front of me.

A horrifying *splat* echoed around me as its upper body was crushed. Bright-red blood and guts seeped out from where its skin had broken, and a foul smell began to spread.

With the exception of the gray skin color, it was mostly the same as a human body. It reminded me of an illustration I had once seen in an anatomy textbook.

The zombie squirmed on the asphalt for a few seconds, then stopped moving. At the very least, that amount of damage seemed to incapacitate it.

I looked up and spotted several zombies on the balcony of an apartment building. They were staring at us, and some leaned over the railing. The zombie that had just been crushed to death seemed to have seen us and jumped.

"Yuuma…"

Hyuuga looked like she was about to start crying as she clung to my arm.

"It's okay. I'm here."

I wouldn't be able to protect her if something as trivial as this was going to upset me. Forcing myself to work up the courage, I stepped into the residential area facing the riverside. We continued down the street at a jog, and it wasn't long before we spotted three male zombies ahead. They began walking in our direction as soon as they saw us.

"Stand back, Hyuuga."

"—Huh?! Aren't we going to run?!"

"There are bound to be more zombies on other streets. Besides, it'll be okay. There aren't that many of them."

I braced myself, then quickly closed the distance between the oncoming zombies and me. Grabbing one by the collar, I threw him into the backyard of a nearby house. A tall fence separated the yard from the road, so I figured he wouldn't be able to scale it right away.

I easily tossed the two remaining zombies into the yard as well. My monstrous zombie strength really did come in handy.

"Hyuuga, let's go."

"Okay!"

Tossing zombies left, right, and center, Hyuuga and I took off at a run, headed for her house. We were almost there when we ran into a miniature horde. There were about ten in all, and taking care of them would require a lot of effort.

"Hyuuga, stay back a sec—" But right then, I saw five zombies I'd just thrown coming toward us.

That wasn't good. I wouldn't be able to protect Hyuuga with enemies on both sides.

I shouldn't have just tossed all those zombies out of our way, but incapacitated them by destroying their upper bodies—an easy enough task with my new zombie strength.

It wasn't too late to start doing that now. I had to stop them completely.

But when I saw the cloudy-white eyes of the zombies staring back at me, I realized I couldn't do it.

The enemies in front of me were shaped like people. They may have been monsters without consciousness, but it wasn't easy to convince myself that it was okay to tear them to pieces when they still looked so human.

What if they regained their self-awareness someday, like I had?

"Yuuma! Over here!"

Hyuuga grabbed my frozen right arm and pulled me onto someone else's property. She opened the front door without a moment's hesitation, and fortunately, it was unlocked. I ran through the house without removing my shoes, then went out through a window in the back. There were no zombies around, and we crossed the yard before the ones from earlier had a chance to catch up.

We'd been running for a little while when Hyuuga came to a stop on a narrow gravel path.

"We should be safe by now, don't you think?"

"Yeah…"

"Let's keep going; my house isn't far from here. It's been five years since you last came over!" Chatting in an incredibly cheerful tone, she set out at a walk again.

"I'm sorry. I couldn't kill those zombies, and I put you in danger," I said, and Hyuuga turned around to face me. "Maybe I'm immortal now, but that doesn't mean anything if I can't fight…"

My chest was burning with shame and regret. I realized that the rules of the world had changed: From this day on, only people who could kill zombies would be able to survive.

It wasn't easy to act rationally, though. I couldn't deny that I didn't want to kill anything that was once a person.

"—Yuuma. You still see people who've become zombies as human beings, don't you?" Hyuuga asked as I stared at the ground.

"…Yeah."

"Then it makes sense that you can't kill them. Don't feel you need to force yourself to; we can keep using our heads to stay away from the zombies."

"…You're sure you don't mind running away, even though I can kill them?"

"Of course I'm sure… That kind heart of yours is one of the things I like best about you," she said with a shy smile.

"…Thanks."

It made me happy that Hyuuga understood my values. I might look like a monster, but that didn't mean I had to be one at heart.

A sense of relief washed over me, and just then, the skin all over my entire body prickled.

*What was that…?*

"—?!! Yuuma, you're…!!"

"Huh?! I'm *what*?"

"How can I explain…? It's faster if you see it for yourself…"

Hyuuga came to stand next to me, then, for some reason, took a photo of us together.

She showed me the screen. My eyes and skin color were back to normal. I looked human again.

"…What's going on?"

"Does this mean you're back to being human?"

"On the outside maybe, but…"

I suddenly realized that my heart was beating again, and warmth had returned to my body.

"Looks like I'm no longer a zombie."

"That's amazing! You did it!"

"I dunno if it's something to get so excited about…"

I'd only been able to fight my way up to here because I'd been a zombie—

"Urrrgh… Aaargh…"

At the worst possible time, we heard zombies moaning again.

A few of them walked slowly toward us, perhaps having overheard our conversation. This wasn't good; I wouldn't be able to protect Hyuuga if I was only human.

But the moment my brain registered the zombies and I adopted a fighting stance, I felt that same prickling sensation as before all over my body.

My arms started turning gray.

"You look like a zombie again!"

"...I have no idea how, but it looks like I'm able to switch back and forth between human and zombie."

Having been through it twice by now, I started getting a feel for the transformation.

I would use this power to do everything I could to protect Hyuuga!!

★ ★ ★

We made it safely through the horde and finally reached Hyuuga's house.

I used to come here every day to play when I was in grade school, so I was bursting with nostalgia, but now was no time to get sentimental.

Hyuuga unlocked the front door and went inside. I followed right behind her, back in my human form.

"I'm home...," Hyuuga called out in a subdued voice, but the house was quiet, with no sign of anyone inside.

Hyuuga forced a smile and said brightly, "I guess no one's home yet. The trains are out, so they must be having a hard time getting home. I'll just wait patiently for them."

"Hyuuga, don't feel you have to put on a brave face. I'll keep an eye out for zombies, so why don't you go lie down for a bit?"

"Mmm... I'm fine. I've been running around a lot, and I'm all sweaty, so what I really want is a shower and a change of clothes. You can take a shower, too, if you want."

"Yeah, that'd be nice."

I'd just been thinking how good it would feel to be clean again. There was no telling how long we'd be able to use the shower, so I should do it while I had the chance.

"You'll want a change of clothes, too, I'd imagine. You're probably about my dad's size. Why don't you try on his clothes?"

"Thanks. I'll take you up on that."

"Come upstairs with me," she said, and we went.

"This place brings back memories..."

I reminisced about the days when I used to come here to play. Takuya's room was at the top of the stairs, Hyuuga's room was down the hallway to the right, and their parents' room was to the left. I could even remember what the inside of each room looked like. Me and Takuya had played here every day after school, but I completely lost contact with him when we started going to different junior high schools.

We didn't have smartphones back then, and I'd thought it inevitable that Takuya would want to start fresh and make new friends. However...

"I'll go and get some of Dad's clothes."

"...Um, Hyuuga, before you do, can I light a stick of incense for him...?"

Hyuuga nodded awkwardly. "Of course. I'm sure it will make him happy." She opened the door to her parents' bedroom.

It was an average Japanese-style room with tatami mats. On the Buddhist altar at the far end of the room was a picture of Takuya.

He would never get any older than he was there, smiling at the camera.

It didn't feel real, seeing his photo. It was as unreal as this zombie-filled world we'd suddenly found ourselves in.

At Hyuuga's prompting, I took a seat in front of the altar. I struck a match, lit a candle, and put a stick of incense to the flame. The burning smell of the incense and its lavender scent tickled my nose.

I put my hands together in front of me, closed my eyes, and apologized to Takuya for not coming to see him until now.

Takuya had died by suicide in his first year of junior high school.

I hadn't been able to accept it at first when my classmates told me about his death. Kids from my sixth-grade class invited me to go with them to pay my respects, but I declined.

In hindsight, I should have said a proper good-bye to Takuya at the time. It had taken me four years to finally pay my respects and offer incense at his altar, and I never would've even come back to this house if my path hadn't crossed with Hyuuga's.

I stood up once I'd finished burning the incense, and Hyuuga, who'd been sitting behind me, bowed her head.

"Thank you."

"I should be the one thanking you. That's been weighing me down for a long time, so I'm glad I finally got to say good-bye."

"That's good… By the way, do you know how my brother died…?"

"…Uh, I heard it was suicide…"

"Yes… It seems my brother got tired of living… He should have just refused to go to school if he hated it… But today, when you told me that you were going to turn into a zombie, I think I understood

a little of how he felt. A person can't live without hope, and sometimes they find that hope in dying…"

"Yeah… I can't tell you how many times it felt like my spirit was
crushed today…"

All the lucky people who'd managed to survive today were probably feeling weak; there was no safe place to hide and no way to get
food. It wouldn't be all that surprising if some people were starting
to think it might be easier to become a zombie.

"…There aren't really that many things I can do, but if I use my
strength as a zombie, I should at least be able to give you a little bit
of hope. First, we'll set up a secure base, then gradually build up
equipment… I'll make you believe tomorrow will be better than
today."

"I look forward to it. I'm counting on you, Yuuma."

Standing there, looking at the thin line of smoke rising from the
incense, we both strengthened our resolve to survive.

That sentimental mood stayed with me for a little while, but soon it
was time to come back to reality.

"Shall we get you a change of clothes and head to the bathroom?"
Hyuuga suggested, opening her father's chest of drawers. She took
out a simple long-sleeved shirt and a pair of stretchy slacks and
handed them to me.

Hyuuga went to her room and quickly selected a change of
clothes, then we headed downstairs. The lights in the bathroom were
on, and the hot water was working, so at least the power and water
still seemed to be functioning.

"Do you want to take the first shower?" Hyuuga asked.

"You can go first, but what are we gonna do if a zombie shows up in the bathroom while you're in there?" I replied.

"Oh good question… Plus, we may not notice a zombie entering the house if the shower's running."

"If anything, it might be drawn by the sound and come crashing in."

"Even just taking a shower can put our lives at risk…"

"We should probably stick close together when one of us is having a shower."

"That sounds a little embarrassing, but I don't see a way around it. When you say, 'close together,' how far away do you mean?"

"Standing in the hallway, maybe? Ideally, I think the changing area would be best."

"Then that's what we'll do. We won't be able to hear each other if we close both the bathroom door and the one to the changing area."

"As long as you're okay with that…"

"Not really, but now isn't the time to be fussy… Okay then, I'm going to get ready to take a shower, so could you turn around?"

"Want me to put on a blindfold?"

"No, I trust you. Besides, it's pointless if you can't see a zombie if one shows up."

"True."

I turned to face the hallway, wondering how things had escalated like this.

"Okay, I'm going to take off my clothes now," Hyuuga announced. Her voice was followed by the sound of rustling fabric.

Staring at the wall connecting the changing room to the hallway, I desperately suppressed my urge to peek.

"…I'm taking off my underwear, so don't you dare turn around."

"I—I won't."

"...I took off my bra."

"Don't give me the play-by-play."

"...That's everything. If you turn around now, you'll see me completely naked."

"Didn't I ask you not to tell me?"

"But it's fun to make you flustered."

"I didn't realize you were so bold. How can you act like that when you aren't wearing anything?"

"Hee-hee. Your voice is trembling. Are you really that interested in my naked body?"

"...If I said yes...would you show it to me?"

"Of course not."

"In that case, not at all."

"Oh reeeally? But you seemed so excited to see my boobs earlier."

"I only asked you to show them to me because I thought I was about to die..."

"So you do want to see my body."

"No comment."

"Hmmm... You know, I was just wondering..."

"You seriously wanna start chatting right now?!"

"Oh, calm down, this won't take long. You really are cute, Yuuma."

"Shut it. Just get to the point."

"You've gone back to human from being a zombie, but does that mean you need to eat now?"

"...Come to think of it, I *am* hungry."

"In that case, I'll fix you a home-cooked meal later on. This is fun, like we're having a cozy date at home. ♪"

"This is no time for you to be enjoying yourself. Do you really think you should be chatting when you're completely naked?"

"Aha. So you *do* believe I'm naked right now."

"What's that supposed to mean?!"

"Seeing as you have such a dirty mind, I thought I'd check to make sure you wouldn't turn around and try to see me naked. I'm actually still wearing my uniform."

"...Right. I was worried for a minute there, thinking you had no sense of shame."

"Well, I'm glad we cleared up that little misunderstanding. Okay then, this time, I'm *really* going to take off my clothes." Once again, I heard the sound of rustling fabric. Thinking back, the noise earlier had seemed too loud, almost as if she'd been doing it on purpose. This time, it was quieter. She must really be taking off her clothes.

Suddenly, Hyuuga seemed to stop moving.

"...Uh-oh. I'm too embarrassed to take off my undies behind you."

"I really wish you wouldn't tell me things like that. How am I supposed to react?"

"Well, I guess there's no rule that says I *have* to get completely nude in the changing room, so I'll take my underwear off in the bathroom."

*"Great idea."*

"I imagine it would be hard for you to stay standing like that the whole time I'm in the shower."

"Yeah, definitely."

"Then feel free to make yourself comfortable. Just don't wander too far away from the changing area. I'll let you know when I'm coming out."

Hyuuga stepped into the bathroom and closed the frosted glass door.

She'd told me to make myself comfortable, but how could I possibly relax in a situation like this…?

I sneaked a glance behind me and could vaguely make out Hyuuga's silhouette as she removed her underwear, leaving her wearing nothing but her birthday suit.

*That…is so hot…!!*

This material of dreams called frosted glass had a magical power that drew a man's gaze and wouldn't let go. You could make out a general picture of the position Hyuuga was in, and you even got sucked into thinking there might be some parts of the glass you could see through.

It was amazing to think that it wasn't a crime to see a girl bathing if you were looking at her through a sheet of frosted glass.

The events from earlier, down by the riverbank, suddenly flashed through my mind, leaving me feeling guilty. But even so, I couldn't take my eyes off her. For about five minutes, I continued to imagine Hyuuga naked, taking a shower on the other side of that frosted glass. I was ashamed of myself, but I guess that's just our nature as guys.

Then the door suddenly started to open, and I quickly turned back around.

"Yuuma, I'd like to get out now, so could you turn around again?"

"I'm not looking in your direction anymore, so don't worry. You can come out."

"You aren't looking *anymore*? So you *have* been looking."

"Don't use those sharp senses of yours on me."

"You're so naughty, Yuuma. You were probably reminiscing about what happened by the river."

"…Sorry."

"There's no need to apologize. The fact that you're so interested in my naked body is proof that you're still you."

"That's gracious of you… But I think the only guy who wouldn't be curious in a situation like this is a killer who lost all his emotions as a child. So forgive me."

"All right. Yuuma…turn around and look at me for a moment."

"…?"

It was a peculiar request, but I turned around anyway—and was shocked by what I saw.

Hyuuga had cracked open the door and was sticking her head and right shoulder out. Right on the other side of the frosted glass was Hyuuga's stark, unclothed figure…and her silhouette was obvious from the neck down.

"…You can't see me, can you?" she asked worriedly, her face red.

"Don't worry, I can't see anything clearly."

My gaze had already traveled several times from the top of the silhouette to the bottom, and I hadn't been able to make out any of the vital details. There was one thing I'd noticed, though…

"Hyuuga, are you not wearing any underwear…?"

The silhouette in front of me didn't make sense unless her underwear was the exact same color as her skin. I couldn't see any bra straps over her shoulders, either…

"I forgot my towel when I got in… I'm really, truly naked now…"

"O-okay…"

"This is mortifying, letting a guy see me nude through the frosted glass. You'll have to do the same thing later."

"No way."

I wouldn't even have the courage to open the door if I was stark naked. There was no doubt Hyuuga was braver than I would be in this situation.

"Anyway, Yuuma, could you bring me the towel on top of the washing machine?"

"S-sure."

"I'll kill you if you try to sneak a peek when you hand it to me."

"Yes, ma'am."

I held out my right hand behind me and gave Hyuuga the towel, facing toward the hallway.

Hyuuga retreated back into the bathroom, wiped herself dry, and put on her clothes. I watched through the frosted glass, thinking about how tough it'd be to put on one of those bras with the hooks in the back.

The door eventually opened again, and Hyuuga stepped out, still drying her wet hair with the towel. She'd changed into a T-shirt and shorts. Hyuuga looked pretty in her school uniform, but she was also surprisingly cute in casual clothes.

"I just realized that, from now on, one of us will always have to be nearby whenever we want to take a bath."

"I guess so."

What a world we were living in now.

"You didn't mind me being here?"

"Of course I *minded* it, but it didn't take too long to get used to—after what happened at the river."

"I—I see…"

"Okay, your turn. I won't peek, so relax and take off all your clothes," Hyuuga said with a smirk.

"…You're gonna turn around and look, aren't you?"

"Huh?! How could you tell?"

"I'm slowly starting to understand you. I think I'll do what you did earlier and take off my clothes in the bathroom."

"Now, just hang on a minute. You saw my breasts when we were down by the river, so don't you think it's only fair that I see you naked, too?"

"...You want to see me naked?"

"I'll *let* you be naked in front of me."

"What's that supposed to mean?!"

Look at her, acting all high and mighty...

"Forget it; you're not allowed to look."

After taking a shower and getting dressed, I went to the kitchen to watch over Hyuuga as she cooked.

"I can't make anything too fancy, so don't get your hopes up."

She put on an apron, opened the refrigerator, and began thinking about what she could make with the ingredients there.

"Is there anything I can do to help?"

"Could you peel some carrots? I'm going to make meat and potato stew." She handed me some washed carrots and a peeler. "I'm not sure about the proper amounts since I always look up the recipe on my tablet when I cook... So cut me some slack if I don't get it right, okay?"

"Of course. It's impressive enough that you can give it a shot without looking at any instructions. Do you cook a lot?"

"Yeah. I make my own lunch almost every day."

"I've got nothing but respect for you doing that. I barely have any cooking experience, so I'll do my best not to get in your way."

"Hee-hee. I've never cooked with anyone besides my mom before, so this is going to be fun. We'll always remember this as the first chore we did together. ♪"

"Wasn't our first joint project burying Takuya's manga in your backyard?"

"Oh yeah. Didn't you want to dig that up?"

"I don't see any point to digging up old manga given our current circumstances. Maybe some other time."

We kept chatting as Hyuuga set the timer on the rice cooker like she knew what she was doing, took the beef out of the freezer, and began defrosting it in the microwave. After finishing peeling the carrots, I watched her deftly cook the beef in a frying pan. Everything she did was perfect, like a scene from a movie.

Hyuuga finished making the meat and potato stew while I stood admiring the scene, and she set it on the table along with a salad she'd had in the refrigerator. The rice finished cooking just in time, too. For dessert, we'd share the pudding I picked up earlier.

We sat facing each other at the table. I took a spoonful of the meat and potato stew and put it in my mouth. Hyuuga waited for my reaction with a nervous expression, and I could feel my back tense up.

I was worried about what to say if it tasted bad, but in the end I didn't have to pretend, since it was genuinely delicious.

"This is great. Like, good enough to serve in a restaurant."

"I'm so glad you like it...," Hyuuga said with a look of relief. "We still have more left in the pot, so feel free to help yourself." She let out a cheerful little giggle. "We're like newlyweds, sitting here eating together."

*Is this amazing or what...?!*

It was an idyllic situation, sitting at the dinner table happily chatting with a beautiful girl. Still, I felt a bit conflicted, since we wouldn't be in this situation if those zombies hadn't appeared...

Eventually we finished our meal, and Hyuuga began washing the dishes.

"So we should figure out what we're gonna do now."

For some reason, Hyuuga looked away in embarrassment.

"...Are you saying you want to be in an intimate relationship with me?"

"That's not what I'm saying *at all*. I'm talking about how we're going to keep this house safe and meet up if we get separated."

"It was misleading, the way you said it!!" Hyuuga almost screamed. She pointed the tip of the knife she was washing toward me, and I raised my hands.

"Was it?"

"Of course it was! Anybody would think a person is professing their love if they said they wanted to 'figure out what *we're* gonna do now.'"

"I think there are other ways to take that..."

"From now on, please don't say *we* when you're talking about making future plans with someone of the opposite sex. It's bound to cause a misunderstanding."

"...O-okay."

It was only after I'd fully accepted her claim that Hyuuga finally lowered the knife.

"Anyway, back to the topic at hand. Let's figure out what to do next. First of all, there's the question of where we're going to sleep tonight."

"I think it's a given that we'll sleep in my room. We'll run into trouble sooner or later if we don't stay together all the time."

"Yeah, guess there's no other way."

"By the way, my room is pretty small, so we'll have to sleep in the same bed."

"...You're good with that?"

"I trust you completely."

"All right, that's settled then. Next on the agenda, how're we gonna find each other if a huge horde of zombies forces their way into the house or something else happens and we get separated?"

"Hmm… Our phones aren't working, and the zombies will flock to us if we shout."

"We should decide on a place to meet up… Where would be best?"

"There's no telling which buildings are still safe."

"I can go out and take a look around, but that creates the problem of what you'll do while I'm gone. It'd be dangerous for you to come with me, and I don't feel safe leaving you here alone, either."

"You're being overprotective, Yuuma. Are you the possessive type with the girls you date?"

"Dunno. I've never had a girlfriend before."

"Ah, I see… Well, I don't particularly mind if you're possessive, so I would much rather stay by your side."

"I don't follow your logic, but all right. Still, you never know what might happen to pull us apart… What I really wanna do is clear all the zombies out of this area we're living in and make it safe…"

"I just thought of something: Isn't it possible to restrain zombies? I don't think we have to force ourselves to kill them, as long as we can keep them quiet."

"Now that you mention it, we should be able to incapacitate them by tying their hands together and sealing their mouths… A zombie's strength is no joke, though, so I don't really know how strong a rope would need to be to keep one from moving."

"Why don't we experiment? You can become a zombie, after all."

"Hyuuga, that's so smart."

And so we decided to test the strength of zombies. After we finished cleaning up the dishes, Hyuuga went to look for something that might be able to restrain a zombie.

"All we have in the house right now is hemp rope for gardening."

The rope she gave me was only about as thick as a phone charging cable, but it was surprisingly sturdy when I tugged on it.

"It might work if we wrap it around a couple of times."

"Let's try it out then. I'll tie you up."

"Okay, tie it around my hands."

"Got it."

I put out my hands, and Hyuuga secured the hemp rope around my wrists. A single loop tore easily due to my monstrous zombie strength, and the same thing happened when she wrapped it around twice.

As we thought, it was gonna take a lot more than that to restrain a zombie. We gradually increased the number of loops and eventually discovered that five times did the trick.

"So now we know we can use rope to restrain the zombies. Okay, untie me."

That was when I saw the dangerous glint in Hyuuga's eyes.

"Hee-hee-hee! You're completely defenseless right now, aren't you?"

"That's not something a young girl should be saying with such glee."

"Can I fool around with you a bit?"

"No way in hell. You're a perv if you like tying up older men."

"Hee-hee-hee. Maybe I am. Tickle, tickle!"

Smiling, Hyuuga slipped her hands beneath my underarms and started wiggling her fingers. But I didn't feel a thing.

"My skin is way less sensitive when I become a zombie. I can sort of feel where you're touching me, but it doesn't tickle."

"Aw, that's no fun."

"Hurry up and untie me."

"Fiiine." Hyuuga pouted and undid the rope.

"By the way, Yuuma, have you ever tied anyone up?"

"Of course not."

"Well then, why don't you practice a little? We can't have you slowing us down when you have to tie up a zombie."

"You mean you want me to tie you up?"

"Yeah, I'll let you practice on me. Go ahead!" she offered with a smile.

I'd somehow gotten permission to tie up Hyuuga. Although I was a little reluctant at first, I knew it was important to practice, so I reached out to bind her hands. But the moment I grabbed Hyuuga's slender wrists, she vigorously shook me off.

"Huh?! Why are you resisting?"

"It's not real practice if I don't resist. That's what zombies would do, right?"

"I guess you've got a point…"

Having been convinced by Hyuuga, I went back to practicing. This time, I bound her wrists together tightly.

"Eek!! Pervert!! Someone help me!!"

"Zombies don't talk, so do you really need to scream?"

"Oh, that's true! Okay, I'll only resist by force."

"You do that."

"Ngh! Hnnngh!"

"Hee-hee-hee. It's no use resisting. You won't get away with a feeble attempt like that."

With a mocking grin, I pushed Hyuuga's wrists together and successfully tied them up.

"*Hmph…* You caught me…"

Having lost the ability to move her hands freely, Hyuuga looked up at me through her lashes. It was a weird feeling… As if I had her under my control.

"…Okay, I'm gonna tie your legs together now."

"Just wait one second. You're looking at me in a lewd way. Are you sure you aren't having dirty thoughts?"

"Of course not. All I'm thinking about right now is how to efficiently immobilize those zombies."

"Really? So you haven't awakened some weird new kink?"

"Rest assured, there's no way I'm gonna develop a thing for tying up young girls."

"If you say so…"

With Hyuuga still looking at me suspiciously, I set my sights on her ankles, but I was worried that if she struggled with her hands tied, she might fall and injure herself.

"I think I'll pass on tying up your feet."

"But you might need to do it when you restrain a zombie."

"True. Well, the way I'd do it would be to first tie up their hands, then knock them over and tie up their feet."

"Is that what you're thinking of doing to me?"

"No, it's dangerous to do that on the floor here. We'd have to try it on a bed."

"Then, are you going to push me down on a bed and tie up my hands and feet?"

"That'd look like something else entirely."

"Then how about this? You princess carry me to the couch, then tie my feet together there."

"I might drop you if you start struggling while I'm carrying you, though."

"I won't. I'll be good."

"But then it wouldn't make for good zombie-restraining practice."

"I'm okay with that. I just want you to carry me like a princess."

"I don't think I understand what you're saying…"

"Don't think too hard about it; just carry me to the couch. Oh, and if you can, don't do it in your zombie form. I want you to do it as a human."

"Huh…? I'm not sure I'll be able to lift you without my zombie strength—"

"Are you saying I look heavy?"

"Not at all. I'm just saying I don't have confidence in my strength."

"You'll be fine. Just do it," Hyuuga demanded with a pout, and I followed her orders.

Who would've thought I'd have the chance to hold a beautiful girl like her in my arms…?

I reverted to human form, then put my left hand against Hyuuga's back, my right hand beneath her knees, and lifted her up in one movement. The next second, her beautiful face was right in front of me. We were so close I could kiss her at any moment.

Our eyes met, and we both immediately turned our heads away. It was too embarrassing to do that at such close range.

Still looking in a different direction, I carried Hyuuga to the sofa, careful not to drop her. Every time I moved, I could feel the sensation and warmth of her body, from her breasts to her thighs, through the thin fabric of her clothes. I was amazed that it wasn't just a girl's breasts that were soft, but her whole body.

Thinking that Hyuuga might sense my wicked feelings if we stayed like this for too long, I quickly put her down on the couch.

"Hee-hee-hee… That was kind of exciting," Hyuuga said with

a smile as she was lying down. She didn't seem to have noticed my dirty thoughts. Maybe I should have enjoyed that sensation a little longer… "I wasn't heavy, was I…?"

"I've never lifted anyone else, so I really couldn't say one way or the other."

"Then you can just assume I'm extremely light."

"O-okay."

I'd been so preoccupied with the fact that her breasts were touching me that I hadn't even thought about her weight… Between that and everything else going on in my brain, I'd almost forgotten we were in the middle of practicing tying up zombies.

I grabbed Hyuuga's legs and quickly bound them with the rope, feeling like I was doing better than I had been before.

"I reckon I'll get the hang of it if we keep doing this."

"You mean you want to keep practicing tying me up?"

"That's a super-misleading question, but yes."

"All right… You'll have to untie the rope first, though."

"Sure."

In the end, I needed to use scissors to cut the rope, since I'd tied it pretty tight. We'd used up more than a meter of rope in one session, so maybe we shouldn't practice too much—

*Bam!!*

A noise suddenly came from the front door, as if something had hit it hard.

"…Yuuma."

"Yeah, it's probably a zombie. I'll go take a look."

I went to the door and looked out through the peephole, but

there was nothing there. Maybe the zombie had moved on or was at an angle I couldn't see.

I wanted to make sure I knew what'd caused the noise, but it would be a pain if I opened the door and a zombie came in—

*Crash!!*

I was mulling over what to do when I heard the sound of glass shattering in the living room where Hyuuga was.

"Aaahh!!"

Hyuuga screamed at almost the exact same time as the noise, and my blood ran cold.

I ran back to the living room to see that the large window facing the yard had been broken, letting in a zombie in a suit. Fortunately, Hyuuga was far away from the window, and she seemed to be unharmed.

I ran over in front of the zombie. Hyuuga stood trembling at my back.

"...D...Dad...," she murmured.

The zombie had been her father.

"Uuurgh... Aaargh..."

Her father turned his lifeless eyes on Hyuuga and let out an indistinct moan.

Overcome with a gloomy sense of despair, I prepared to fight— but it made no move to attack me. Still, it wasn't as if it had any sense of who he was...

"Dad...," Hyuuga mumbled with a dazed expression. She took a step closer toward her father.

The zombie bared its gums menacingly, saliva dripping from between sharp teeth.

Yet it still didn't attack. It looked straight at Hyuuga, its entire body convulsing.

I couldn't be sure, but it seemed to be resisting the urge to attack us.

"Do you think there could still be a tiny bit of your dad's will inside it...? Maybe he's fighting against his zombie instinct to attack you."

His suit and leather shoes were covered in mud. Hyuuga's dad must've been so worried about his family that he had desperately rushed home, but somewhere along the way, he'd been bitten by a zombie.

"...Yuuma. Can I give Dad a hug?" Hyuuga asked tearfully as she and the zombie continued to stare at each other. "He doesn't seem to recognize me when I call out to him, but I want him to feel my warmth, so he knows I'm okay."

"...Right now, I think your dad's caught in a tug-of-war between his zombie instincts and his own will. There's no telling which is gonna win out if we get any closer."

"Please. I can't just leave him like this."

"...All right. But be careful."

"I will...!!"

Hyuuga wiped away her tears and thrust her arms forward, a determined look on her face. Closing the distance between her and her dad, she gingerly put her arms around him.

"—Raaargh!!"

The moment their bodies came into contact, the zombie's eyes flashed open and it bared its teeth, trying to bite Hyuuga's shoulder. I quickly pushed my right arm in front of its face, letting it bite me instead, and a row of sharp teeth sank into my forearm. Blood spurted from the wound; I thought my arm would be torn off if I relaxed my muscles.

"Yuuma!!"

"I'm all right. Don't worry about me; talk to your dad."

"Okay…"

Hyuuga squeezed her arms around her dad, holding him tighter.

"I'm okay, Dad. Yuuma protected me."

"…Uuurgh…"

"You came home because you were worried about me, didn't you? Thank you. I've got Yuuma with me, and he's going to protect me now, so you don't have to worry. Dad… I love you." Hyuuga's voice was a whisper, and a single tear rolled down her cheek.

That was when the strength went out of her dad's bite. A voice escaped his mouth, so faint I thought it might fade away into nothingness.

"…Ha…ru…ka…"

The zombie suddenly lost all its strength and fell to the ground. Hyuuga cried out timidly, calling for her father, but there was no response. Her dad's eyes were closed, and he remained completely still.

We examined her dad's body and found that his heart had stopped, he wasn't breathing, and that there was no warmth to it. His skin was still gray, though, so that didn't necessarily mean he was dead.

After talking it over, Hyuuga and I decided to let him sleep in the bedroom on the first floor. We didn't know if he'd wake up, and even if he did, he might be a full-blown zombie. Still, we felt bad about restraining him, so in the end, we decided just to keep a close eye on him.

We double-checked to make sure he wasn't responding to

sounds or vibrations, then we left the bedroom. Hyuuga's legs shook as she walked in front of me.

"Hyuuga, are you okay?"

"Sorry… I'm just a little tired."

"I don't blame you. Your dad's become a zombie…"

"Yeah… But that doesn't mean he's *completely* transformed into a zombie yet, right…?" Hyuuga seemed to be begging for hope as she looked at me with that searching gaze. "Maybe he'll wake up one day and be able to talk like you…"

"…Yeah."

I felt like there was a good chance of that. He'd clearly been acting different than the other zombies I'd seen.

"So let's not make this situation any glummer than it has to be," Hyuuga said. "Dad loved it when things were lively; he might hear us laughing and wake up if we're enjoying ourselves…"

I didn't want to get her hopes up too high, but I decided to share my hypothesis with Hyuuga.

"You saw that zombie jump from the balcony when we were walking near that apartment building, right?"

"—Huh? …Oh yeah."

"There were other zombies out there on that balcony, but they only watched us and didn't jump. So what if—and this is a big *if*—each zombie's purpose is different? Some zombies might be hellbent on attacking humans, while others might not be so active, like your dad. He still wasn't aware of who he was, but it was almost like he had a purpose that was more important than attacking people…"

"What sort of purpose…?"

"Your dad was probably wishing he could see his family the moment he turned. It was because he had that strong motivation that he became different from the average zombie. And maybe he stopped functioning because he was satisfied after seeing you and achieving that purpose."

"That makes sense… I hope he can go back to being himself, the way you did…" Her voice was weak, and she seemed exhausted.

"Hyuuga, don't you think you should rest a while?"

"I have to clean up that broken glass in the living room. It's dangerous…"

"I hate to say this, but we have to move to someplace safer. We can't use your house as a base if zombies can break the windows and get in."

"Right… Then we'd better get going."

"It's almost nightfall, and it's dangerous to walk around in the dark. We'll set out in the morning, so get some rest while you can."

"Thanks… What about you, though…?"

"I'm fine. Maybe it's because I'm a zombie, but I'm not the least bit tired. I'll keep watch on the first floor, so you just relax and go to bed."

"All right… I'll do that. But if anything happens, don't hesitate to wake me up." Hyuuga sounded a little more relieved than she had earlier, and she slowly went up the stairs.

Now that I was alone, I went to the living room and cleaned up the broken glass, cut pieces of the hemp rope into appropriate lengths, and did whatever else I could to prepare.

About five hours later, a little after eleven, Hyuuga woke up and carefully made her way down the stairs in the pitch-dark house. I got up from the couch in the living room and went to check on her.

"…You're here in my home," she murmured, "which means

everything that's happened since this morning wasn't a dream." A troubled expression crossed Hyuuga's face.

"Sadly not. It's all real—the world's been overrun by zombies."

"For some reason, I keep thinking about the day my brother died. No matter how my parents explained it, I just couldn't believe it was real; it was like a thick fog had enveloped my mind. I collapsed on my bed and fell asleep, and when I woke up in the morning, my head was clear. But my brother was still gone, and I had no choice but to accept it was real... Sorry, I'm darkening the mood. Not only have you been bitten by a zombie, but you haven't found your family..."

"It's okay. Did you get some rest?"

"Yeah, all thanks to you. Are you sure you don't need to lie down?"

"Actually, I am starting to feel a little drowsy."

"Then go upstairs and get some sleep. I'll stay up and wake you if anything happens," she said, playfully flexing a bicep. I was glad she seemed to be feeling a bit more energetic than earlier.

"Okay, I think I will."

"Right this way, please."

I followed Hyuuga up the stairs, and she led me into her bedroom. The room was dimly lit with only a night-light.

"You can use my bed."

"...You're sure?"

"Hmm? Is there a problem?"

"I dunno if I'd call it that. It's just—I'm a boy, and you're a girl..."

"We don't have any other bedding you can use, though. Dad's in the bedroom on the first floor, and it's been a long time since anyone's used Takuya's bed, so I don't feel comfortable having a guest sleep in it..."

"Well, I'm okay with it if you are."

"...? Why wouldn't I be?"

"I didn't think girls liked having other people use their bed."

"That's true, but I don't mind at all if you're the one in it," she said with a bright smile. There wasn't a hint of concern in her expression; it seemed she really didn't mind if I slept in her bed and wasn't just saying that to be kind.

"I'll take you up on your offer, then."

Having been given permission to use her bed, I went to lie down on it in front of Hyuuga. Her sweet scent wafted from the pillow and the blanket, making me feel strangely nervous...

I stopped thinking for a moment and tried to close my eyes.

All I could make out in the darkness were the faint sounds of the two of us breathing. I'd probably be able to fall asleep if I stayed like this for a while.

...But as I lay still, I couldn't help but remember everything I'd been through today.

Zombies had bitten all my classmates, and when I went back home, I'd seen the same thing had happened to my family... I still didn't know if my dad and other relatives were okay, but I probably shouldn't get my hopes up... And who knew when I might lose the ability to think like a human being...?

I opened my eyes, no longer able to bear the horror of it all, and my gaze met Hyuuga's.

"Oh, sorry. Is it hard for you to sleep with me watching you?"

"...No, it's not that..." I found myself at a loss for words, but she seemed to understand how I felt.

"I get it. It's only natural to worry about your family and stuff..."

"...Yeah. I know there's no use thinking about it, though...," I murmured, gazing up at the ceiling.

Then Hyuuga asked hesitantly, "…Um, Yuuma. Am I a burden on you?"

"…What?"

"I mean, what you really want to do is go and check on your family and see if they're okay, right? If you were alone, you could move around freely, but you can't do that now because you have me to protect—"

"That's not true!" I pulled myself up and vehemently denied what she'd said. "It's true I'm worried about everyone's safety, but you aren't a burden on me at all. In fact, you being here *saved* me; I'm pretty sure it was thanks to you that I didn't get completely zombified in the first place. The moment I turned, I had this powerful urge to protect you. So…please, don't ever think again that you're a burden on me."

"Yuuma… Thank you…" Tears glistened in her eyes, seemingly out of relief.

"Hyuuga, I'm sorry I sounded so negative. It can't be helped to some extent, considering the state of the world we're in, but let's try not to think about it. It's better to be constructive, like going over what we'll do when morning comes."

"I understand; I'll try not to. Um… I'll make us breakfast in the morning, since there are still some vegetables and a few other things in the refrigerator."

"Great. I'll have to go out and look for food supplies after that."

"I can't go with you, can I?"

"I don't think so… It'd be best if you waited someplace safe, but is there anywhere like that now…?"

"A regular house won't do, huh?"

"No. Ideally, it'd be a building surrounded by a fence…"

"Then how about the dorm at my high school? It's an all-girls school, and I went to look around it once. I'm pretty sure they have a fence around the dormitory to keep out intruders."

"Sounds good. Let's check it out."

"Is there anything else we should do now while we have the chance?"

"Considering our plan to combat the zombies, I've been thinking we need more defensive gear. I really wish we could find you some metal armor—"

"Armor seems like it would be heavy, though, and I probably couldn't run wearing it."

"Yeah, true. Then how about some sort of gauntlets?"

"What are they?"

"Like armored gloves that cover your arms from fingertips to elbow. You could fend off an attacking zombie if your arms were protected, right?"

"Oh, that makes sense. But where could we find something like that?"

"...I don't know." I'd never needed gauntlets before, so I had no idea where we'd find a pair. It wasn't like we could look it up on a phone, either...

"Let's see if we can't come up with a way to make one," I suggested.

Talking with Hyuuga like this, it was almost as if all the negative emotions swirling around in my chest were gradually being cleansed. We could lament the state of the world all we wanted, but it wouldn't go gentle on us. We had to grit our teeth and keep on living.

...That said, as a zombie, I wasn't sure if I could say I was actually living.

# DAY 2

I opened my eyes to a dark room and realized I must've woken up before dawn. When my brain caught up a moment later, I remembered I wasn't sleeping in my bed.

I immediately pulled myself up and locked eyes with Hyuuga, who was sitting nearby.

"Good morning, Yuuma."

"...If you're here, Hyuuga, then that means I wasn't dreaming."

"See, that's a perfectly normal reaction, waking up to this."

"Well, yeah, considering what a crazy place this world's suddenly become..."

I wished it had all just been a dream. To think that my friends, family—everyone I knew and loved had become zombies...

—No, snap out of it! It was only just last night I made up my mind not to be so pessimistic.

"How long was I asleep?"

"About five hours. You can go back to sleep if you're still tired."

"Nah, I'm okay. My head feels a lot clearer now."

"Good. Let me give you an update on our current situation: Dad still seems to be sleeping, no zombies have shown up since last time, and my phone still isn't getting a signal."

"Okay. I guess we should be happy things haven't gotten worse…"

Having come to accept reality, I went down to the first floor followed by Hyuuga, who was going to make us breakfast.

"Do you usually eat Western- or Japanese-style breakfasts?"

"My family has Japanese-style breakfasts, though most of the time I just feel like a slice of bread…"

"It's really best to eat a substantial breakfast. Miso soup is especially good since it's full of nutrients. You should also be eating fermented foods like yogurt or natto."

"You sound like my mom."

"From today on, I'll look after all your nutritional needs. Just leave it to me!" Hyuuga said, puffing out her chest proudly.

She started preparing breakfast for us, skillfully slicing up a leek and tofu, then simmering them in a pot. While she was cooking, I used a few pieces of cardboard that Hyuuga had brought me to seal up the broken window. Even though we'd be leaving this place soon, I didn't want to go without patching things up.

Once I'd managed to finish fixing up the window, I saw Hyuuga carrying a wide variety of dishes into the dining room, including rice, natto, miso soup filled with all sorts of different ingredients, grilled salmon, fried eggs and bacon, and boiled mustard greens. There was so much food it was hard to believe we were currently fighting for our lives.

"I wanted to use up as many of the ingredients in the fridge as possible. We still have a lot of eggs left, so I think I'll make omelets and pack them for our lunch. Do you like your omelets sweet or savory?"

"Sweet, please."

Impressed by Hyuuga's housekeeping skills, I dug into the breakfast she'd prepared.

Once our bellies were full, we were finally ready to head to the girls' dormitory. Hyuuga changed into her school uniform so anybody would immediately recognize her as a student there, and she also began to write a note to her mother for when she returned home. Meanwhile, I filled a backpack with preserved foods and snacks I'd found in the house.

Hyuuga finished writing her note and turned to me. "Hey, we're driving to the dorm, right?" she asked, as if it were already decided.

I wasn't comfortable driving without a license, but we didn't have any other safe way to get there.

"Hyuuga, do you know how to start a car?"

"I think so. I always used to sit in the passenger seat and watch my dad and my grandpa drive."

"Then it's all yours. I don't know the first thing about driving…"

"Okay."

With that settled, I gathered up all the food and clothes we needed and put them in the trunk and back seat of the car.

Just as we were ready to leave, Hyuuga said she wanted to see her dad, so we went together to the bedroom, where he was still fast asleep. Hyuuga sat on the bed, pulled back the comforter, and held his hand.

"…Bye, Dad. I'll be back."

I sat up straight beside her, hearing the pain in Hyuuga's voice.

"I promise I'll protect Haruka," I told her dad. "We'll make sure to come back every now and then to check in on you, so relax and rest up."

Hyuuga's eyes widened hearing me say that, and she smiled shyly. "It sounds like I'm leaving home to be your bride."

"I wish you'd stop saying things I don't know how to react to when we're right next to your sleeping dad."

"It's okay. I'm sure he'd congratulate me if he heard."

"You think...? I doubt any father would be comfortable seeing his daughter get all mushy with a guy..."

"Then maybe that would wake him up. You know, my heart skipped a beat hearing you call me by my first name. Call me Haruka from now on."

"Please do *not* start acting all mushy," I told her. On the inside, though, I was relieved to see Hyuuga acting more like herself.

I didn't know what her dad's condition was, but I hoped that someday he'd be able to live the same sort of life I had now...

"So shall we get going?" Hyuuga got to her feet and walked toward the doorway.

Looking all around us, we stepped out of the house and got in the car. Hyuuga sat in the driver's seat, and she turned on the engine.

"We're in luck! There's more than half a tank of gas left."

"You know how to read the gas gauge?"

"My grandfather taught me. Now then, next stop, the girls' dormitory!"

"Please drive carefully."

"You worry too much, Yuuma. And even if we *did* get into an accident, you wouldn't die because you're a zombie."

"I don't care about me; I wouldn't want anything happening to you."

"I wish you wouldn't catch me off guard, saying nice things like that."

"I promised your father I'd protect you."

"What you *actually* said was, 'I promise I'll protect Haruka.' Aren't you going to call me by my first name from now on?"

"Huh? You were serious about that?"

"Of course I was serious. We're not going anywhere until you call me by my first name."

"That's gonna be a problem…"

"Then hurry up and call me Haruka. This car isn't moving an inch until you do."

"…Haruka."

"Hee-hee-hee, thank you. Okay, time to go. Oh, and just so you know, the car might come to a sudden stop if you call me by my surname, so I'd watch out if I were you. ♪"

Hyuuga—or rather, Haruka, giggled like a naughty child as she worked the stick shift, and we slowly moved forward.

I couldn't believe the situation I'd found myself in. Here I was, sitting in the passenger seat of a car, with a high school girl younger than me driving.

With a serious look on her face the whole time, Haruka maneuvered the steering wheel and succeeded in getting us out of the garage.

"Amazing! I turn the wheel, and the car goes the same way…!" Haruka exclaimed excitedly as she drove around the zombies that had been drawn to the sound of the engine. "This is so much fun! It's just like a game!"

"You almost seem too good at this. Is it really your first time driving?"

"It's surprisingly easy. You can try it later, too," Haruka said happily as she made her way through the backstreets and out onto the main road.

The area was in a dreadful state. Burned-out, crashed cars littered the road as far as the eye could see, and zombies roamed everywhere in between. They came at us all at once, so we drove in the opposite lane, ignoring the road rules. But in a lot of places, multicar collisions had blocked traffic completely, in which case Haruka would drive around them, or I'd get out of the car and physically remove the obstacles.

Our entire trip continued just like that, taking a lot of effort even to move forward just a few meters...

It took a long time, but we finally made it to the girls' high school that Haruka attended. We parked a little ways away, since the sound of a car engine would attract zombies, and walked to the dorm from there.

Restraining all the zombies we ran into along the way, we passed the grounds of Haruka's old school. I saw a considerable number of zombies when I took a look around, and I couldn't help but wonder whether Haruka's friends were among them...

About a minute later, we spotted the dorm. There were no zombies inside the fence, and I could feel my heart racing with anticipation. However, the entrance gate was locked, and we needed a key to enter.

"How are we going to get inside?" Haruka asked. I took another good look at the steel fence in front of us; it was probably just over two meters tall, with no crossbars I could use as footholds. If I was solo, I would've been able to turn into a zombie to boost my strength and climb the fence... But I couldn't leave Haruka alone.

"What if we brought the car here and climbed on top of it?" I suggested.

"Then we'd have to leave it where it was, and a passing zombie might use it to climb the fence the same way."

"Yeah, you're right. If only there was a ladder… There's no way we'd get that lucky, though."

"We don't have much time. What if one of us gave the other a boost?"

"…That's probably the quickest way. You'd climb on top of me, right?"

"Yeah. Why do you look so happy about that?" Haruka stared at me suspiciously. She seemed to have noticed me glancing at her skirt just now, but I figured I'd play innocent.

"I'm not happy about anything."

"For your information, I'm wearing leggings underneath, so it won't matter if you see up my skirt."

"What?! You are?"

"Disappointed?"

"Not at all. If anything, I'm relieved."

"Should I take off my leggings so you can peek?"

"N-no, you don't have to do that…"

"Of course, I'm kidding. Don't get so flustered."

"…Just hurry up and climb on my shoulders."

I feigned calm and squatted in front of the fence.

"…Okay, here goes." A hint of embarrassment had crept into Haruka's voice, and she placed a leg on my right shoulder. Next, she put her other leg on my left shoulder, and I felt her whole weight on me.

I couldn't believe what was happening. My head was sandwiched between Haruka's thighs, and her skirt fluttered against the back of my neck. The sight and sensation were too good to put into words, but now wasn't the time to dwell on it.

I shook off my evil thoughts and tried to stand up, but the awkward movements made me lose balance.

"—Whoa!"

Haruka clung to my shoulders, and something soft pressed against the top of my head. It was a different type of softness from her thighs.

…Judging by her position, it must have been her boobs…

Overjoyed, I quickly got to my feet and stood against the fence.

"Think you can climb over now?"

"Yeah. I can reach the top."

Haruka's milky-white thighs brushed against my cheeks as she began to move upward. The moment she raised herself up, the hem of her skirt fluttered before my eyes, and something else soft touched the top of my head.

"—Ah!" Haruka let out a panicked cry and clung to the fence.

With those slender arms of hers, she was going to have a hard time pulling herself over.

"Yuuma, can you push me from below?"

"You got it."

I grabbed the soles of her shoes, which fluttered in the air, and gave them one big push. Haruka's upper body went over the fence; it looked like she wouldn't have a problem making it to the other side.

Just so you know, from that angle I could see all the way up her skirt, and even with leggings, it was still an exciting sight to behold.

I couldn't help but keep thinking…it had been her bottom that had brushed the top of my head a minute ago. While I'd been letting my mind run wild with all sorts of lewd thoughts, Haruka had managed to land safely on the other side of the fence. Now, it was my turn.

"—Stop right there!"

A shrill voice suddenly yelled out from somewhere close by, and I froze to the spot. Seconds later, a girl wearing a traditional Japanese *hakama* appeared from inside the building and drew her bow on me.

"I'm sorry, but to avoid any trouble, this dormitory is closed to men. The girl is allowed in, however, you are not permitted on these grounds." The young woman had waist-length brown hair and was glaring at me; one wrong move, and I was sure she'd shoot.

For now, I raised my hands and tried negotiate with her.

"I'm not armed, and I don't intend to harm you, either. Seeing as how we've both managed to survive this far, can't we try to cooperate?"

"Unfortunately, I must decline."

"We have the means to procure food and other necessities."

"There will be no negotiating, as I can't verify that you are, in fact, telling the truth."

"Would you believe me if I brought you some food?"

"We have food stocked inside the dormitory. I cannot take any risks, seeing as I don't know who you are or your intentions."

The girl continued to reject my suggestions, keeping her bow drawn the whole time. She seemed incredibly wary of me, just based on the fact that I was male. I guess I couldn't blame her, though, since the police weren't around anymore…

Yet despite her stern tone, I could see the hesitancy in her expression; she must be feeling guilty about having to turn me away. In

that case, maybe it was better to withdraw, rather than continue to press the issue and rub her the wrong way.

"I understand. I'll give up on entering the building. Just let me make sure of one thing first: You don't have a problem letting Haruka stay here, do you?"

"Of course not. She seems to be a student here, so we can trust her."

"Good..."

I hadn't expected things to turn out like this, but there was some good to come out of it. I could leave Haruka here and go off by myself to collect supplies.

Just as that thought went through my mind, Haruka's eyes met mine.

"Yuuma, I hope you're not even *considering* leaving me here."

"I'll come and get you when I find someplace safe for us. Besides, I'll be back once a day to bring you supplies, and—"

"No." Her tone said it was out of the question. "If you can't stay here, then neither will I."

"...I'm worried about taking you with me to places we don't know are safe. I'll go alone and check things out first, then come back."

"All you have to do is protect me."

"Stop being unreasonable. I promised your dad you'd be safe with me."

"You did, so don't go back on your word now. What if zombies are lurking somewhere in this dorm?"

"—Oh. Now that you mention it, that is a possibility..."

Haruka was right: It was dangerous to leave her here without checking that the place was safe first.

Listening to our exchange, the girl with the bow and arrow put down her weapon and turned to Haruka.

"What do you want to do? I'll open the gate for you if you wish to leave."

"Please, let me out. I don't want to stay here by myself."

"Understood. I'll unlock the gate—but *you*," she said, looking at me. "Don't you dare try to slip in when I open it. I'll shoot you if I see you making any strange moves." She repositioned her arrow on the bowstring and continued to regard me suspiciously.

"I won't… Oh, and let me know if you need anything in the way of supplies," I told her. "We're going to the supermarket later, so I'll pick them up while we're there."

"—Huh?" I seemed to have caught the girl by surprise, because her eyes widened, just for a moment. "…Why would you offer to do something like that?"

"What d'you mean, 'why'? We all need food, don't we?"

"That's not what I meant… Why would you even consider helping out someone who rejected you…?" the girl asked, sounding confused. She really didn't seem to get why I was offering to help her out.

*…Oh right. I'm resistant to zombies, so it's natural for me to want to help, but other people wouldn't have the luxury to do that…*

"Aaargh…"

I suddenly heard a zombie moaning behind me. Turning around, I saw it was wearing the same uniform that Haruka had on. It had probably wandered close after hearing our conversation.

"—Oh no!" The girl immediately took out a key, unlocked the gate, and shouted, "Quick, get inside!"

"No; you said guys weren't allowed inside, so you can't let me in." I picked up a rock about the size of a fist and shoved it into the zombie girl's mouth as she tried to bite me. I swiftly went around her and tied her hands behind her back, but in the process, the rock fell out of her mouth. The girl flailed violently, trying to sink her teeth into me.

This was one ferocious zombie; simply restraining her hands and feet might not be enough. I wanted to secure her someplace where it wouldn't matter if she thrashed about...

Looking around, I spotted a telephone pole. Something like that wouldn't break, even if the zombie went wild.

Not wanting to scare the girls in the dorm, I dragged the zombie about ten meters away, then used the hemp rope to tie her neck to the pole. The girl zombie bared her teeth and tried to bite me. I watched her for a little while, but she didn't seem to be clever enough to free her arms and neck from the rope.

Satisfied, I returned to the girls' dorm and saw the young woman in the *hakama* frozen on the spot behind the half-open gate.

"...Aren't you afraid of the zombies?"

I didn't quite know how to respond to that. I could tell her it wasn't a problem if a zombie bit me, but that might mean I'd have to leave Haruka here at the dorm. It was probably better to hide the fact that I was...*different*.

"I am scared, but I'm more afraid of zombies biting other people."

That must be how the average person felt when they confronted a zombie. Not that I knew.

"...Answer me one more question: Why didn't you kill it? Destroying its head would have reduced the risk of it biting you, rather than just tying it up."

"True, but what if there's a way to turn the zombies back into human beings again? I don't want to have any regrets if we ever find a way to do that."

The truth was that I didn't have the guts to kill a zombie, but I tried playing it a bit cool.

A resolute look appeared on the girl's face, and she opened the gate.

"Forgive my earlier rudeness. Please come in; you're welcome to live in the dormitory here."

"—Huh? But I thought guys weren't allowed."

"The reason we refuse entry to men is because I'm still too inexperience to discern whether they will cause problems. It's my duty to protect the girls here, so I've had to be very strict in dealing with the current situation. You seem sincere, though, so I think we'll be safe letting you in. There is still a chance that something might happen, but having witnessed your courage, I've decided that the potential returns of letting you join our community outweigh the risks.

"...I've tried not to show any weakness, but the fact is we have no means of procuring food. Even if we continue to keep ourselves locked up here, the only future we have to look forward to is starving to death... However, if you're truly able to obtain food as you claim you are, we may yet be able to survive." The girl looked straight at me, her eyes filled with hope. "My name is Mai Tsukishiro. I'm a third-year student here."

"Uh, I'm Yuuma Kousaka. I'm in second year."

We were introducing ourselves as if it were completely normal, when Haruka interrupted.

"I'm Haruka Hyuuga, a first-year student. Oh, and by the way, Yuuma's crazy in love with me, so you don't have to worry about him fooling around with other girls. Isn't that right, Yuuma?" Haruka had asked the question in an innocent tone of voice, tilting her head slightly, but her eyes weren't smiling.

"O-of course."

"I'll be responsible for keeping an eye on him twenty-four seven, from morning until night, so you won't have to worry about a thing," Haruka said, puffing out her ample chest.

Tsukishiro chuckled. "All right. Nice to meet you, Kousaka and Hyuuga. We'll be counting on you both from here on out."

With introductions over, Tsukishiro went inside the dorm building and returned once she'd told the other survivors what had happened.

"Thank you for waiting. I told the other two girls here about you, and they agreed to let you use the building."

That meant we now had everyone's permission to stay here. I felt a wave of relief, since there was all the possibility in the world they would simply have rejected me.

"Do all the survivors here go to this high school?"

"Yes. There's Lisa Hoshimiya, a third-year student, and Ayumi Ichinose from second year. Hoshimiya doesn't have the best attitude; she skipped school yesterday to play video games in her room, which saved her from running into zombies. Ichinose, on the other hand, is very studious. She was sick with a cold yesterday, which is how she avoided the zombies. She's shy, though, so it may take a while for her to open up to you…"

"That's okay. I'll try to give her as much space as possible."

"Thank you. One more thing… I'm sorry to ask this of you, but would you mind checking the dorm to see if there are any zombies inside? I should really be the one to do it, but I can't leave the gate area."

"No problem. In fact, I was going to ask if I could do that."

And so Haruka and I went off to inspect all the rooms to see if any zombies were lurking there.

According to Tsukishiro, the dorm was five stories tall with a total of fifty rooms, each of which housed two students, with two desks and a bunk bed. We started at the end of the hall on the ground floor and checked each room, looking in the closets, under the beds, and any other places big enough for a person to hide.

Almost all the rooms were cluttered with girls' belongings, since they'd still been using them right up until yesterday morning. Underwear was strewn about in some places, but I had to be the first to enter as long as there was a possibility of zombies lurking about. I checked each room mechanically, doing my best not to look any more than necessary.

"...Yuuma. Do you really think there's a chance that zombies might be hiding in here somewhere?" Haruka asked after we'd inspected twenty rooms or so. It sounded like she'd already gotten bored. "Tsukishiro and the other girls slept here last night. Wouldn't they have already run into zombies if they were still here?"

"Not necessarily. For example, there's the possibility that someone might have gotten bit, come running in here, hidden under a bed, and only then turned into a zombie. Maybe they haven't been able to crawl out."

None of the zombies we'd run into so far had been very intelligent; it wouldn't be surprising if one or two were still in here, unable to move.

"And that zombie might free itself at some point and attack a survivor. Hey, weren't you the one who said zombies might be here in the first place?"

"That was just something I said on the spur of the moment to stop you from leaving me here."

"Ah, I see. Still, even if there's only a one percent chance this place isn't totally safe, I won't be able to relax unless I finish checking all the rooms."

We continued sweeping the dorm until we finally arrived at

Ayumi Ichinose's room on the fourth floor. I didn't see a need to check it for zombies, but I figured we should say hi to her anyway. When I knocked, a faint reply came from inside, and the door opened a crack. The security chain was still attached as a short girl with dark hair peeked out with a fearful expression.

"Hi, I'm Yuuma Kousaka. This is Haruka Hyuuga. We'll be staying here in the dorm with you starting today, so I thought we'd come by and say hello."

"Oh... Yes... Tsukishiro told me about you...," Ichinose replied in a whisper, her eyes focused somewhere off in the distance. She looked frightened, like a small animal that had stumbled across its natural predator.

"By the way, I heard you had a cold yesterday. Please don't hesitate to let me know if you need any medicine or vitamin drinks."

Ichinose's expression seemed to soften a little. "Thank you, but I've already recovered..."

"You have? That's good to hear... We better go, then. It was nice meeting you."

"Thank you. Thank you so much..." Ichinose bowed so many times I thought she might break her neck, and Haruka and I went back to checking the area.

We finished inspecting the first four floors, then went up to Lisa Hoshimiya's room on the fifth. The door opened as soon as I knocked, and a beautiful girl with blond hair appeared.

"Hi, sorry to bother you. I'm—"

"Oh, Tsukishiro told me about you! Nice to meet you!" the girl said cheerfully, opening the door wide. I got a view of her incredible figure. She was dressed in a black camisole, which involuntarily drew my eyes to her chest.

*...She might have even bigger boobs than Haruka...*

"*Ahem.*"

Standing behind me, Haruka coughed. How had she known what I was thinking when she couldn't even see my face from there? "I'm Lisa Hoshimiya. You're Kousaka, right? I heard you tied up a zombie. That's amazing."

"Oh, uh, I mean…"

"So far, I've only ever seen zombies from a distance. Tsukishiro says it's dangerous and won't let me leave the dorm. I skipped class yesterday and stayed in my room to play video games, but then, all of a sudden, the internet dropped out and I couldn't get back online. So I was lying on my bed, feeling all annoyed, when I heard something that sounded like a scream and rushed downstairs. That's when Tsukishiro came running back to the dorm and locked the gate."

Hoshimiya excitedly yammered on, then looked at me with a serious expression.

"Y'know, I still find it hard to believe, but are they really zombies? Do they try to bite you like in the movies?"

"Yep; they thrash around like crazy trying to get their teeth in you."

"Oh yeah…? I wonder if everyone at school is okay…," she said, sounding concerned. I was sure Tsukishiro had tried to spare them most of the details, so I decided not to tell Hoshimiya that her school had been full of zombies when I'd passed by there earlier.

"By the way… Kousaka. Is it true that you might go out looking for food for us…?"

"Yeah, that's the plan."

"Wow, you're so brave! I'm seriously counting on you!"

Hoshimiya reached out and wrapped both her hands around my right fist like she was pleading. From where she was standing, I must have looked like a savior. I wasn't sure how to react, though—after all, I had a secret advantage: the ability to turn into a zombie.

As we left her room, I thought about how happy it made me to get such a warm welcome. But the moment Hoshimiya closed her door, Haruka pushed me against the wall and began her interrogation.

"You were staring at her breasts, weren't you?"

"Wh-what're you talking about?"

"So anybody will do, as long as they've got big boobs?"

"No, it's not like that…"

"Then, is it because she's beautiful?"

"……"

"*Hmph…*" Haruka pouted as I struggled over how to answer.

"Hey, I can't help it if my eyes are drawn there. It's just instinct."

"And after I let you feast your eyes on *my* boobs…"

"I can't say anything to that."

"I'll forgive you if you promise never to look at her chest again."

"…I'll do my best to avoid having her in my line of sight."

"I appreciate your honesty, but don't think you're going to get away with this by just admitting everything."

"I mean, it's gonna be practically impossible to avoid seeing her when we're living in the same dorm…"

"You're a zombie, so I'm pretty sure you'll be okay if I crush your eyes, right?"

"Absolutely not."

I wished she wouldn't say such scary things… But this was no time for idle chatter, so we shelved the issue for now and resumed our inspection.

We continued checking the dorm, but in the end, our fears were unfounded. We searched everywhere, including the kitchen and the bathrooms, but didn't find a single zombie.

Now that we could relax on the zombie front, we decided to go and get the car. I went alone to where we'd parked and tried to drive it back, recalling how Haruka had done it.

Driving was more difficult than I'd expected. I had trouble with every part of it—knowing the amount of pressure to use on the accelerator, figuring out the angle I needed to turn the steering wheel, checking behind the car when driving in reverse—and was seriously impressed by how easy Haruka had made it look.

I gave myself plenty of time and eventually managed to drive back to the dorm, then carried all our belongings inside and prepared to venture out to a nearby supermarket.

"Are you sure you don't mind going…?" Tsukishiro asked me seriously when I told her I was heading out for supplies. "You don't have to go today… We can survive for at least a week with what we have now."

Tsukishiro was looking out for me, hoping I would stay alive as long as possible. It was only natural for her to react like that, since she believed she was sending me out into a life-or-death situation.

"Don't worry, I'll come back alive for sure. And if I'm going out at some point, I might as well do it before fresh foods go bad."

"All right… I'll pray for your safe return…"

She bowed deeply, making me feel guilty about lying to her as I got in the car.

At that moment, I saw Haruka walk out of the building.

"Have you come to see me off?"

"Yeah. Get out there and steal lots of food for us."

"The way you say that…"

"It sounds like so much fun, going on a stealing spree in a deserted supermarket."

"…If I can make sure the supermarket's safe, do you wanna come with me later?"

"Absolutely! I can't wait to go looting with you!"

"There's seriously something wrong with the way you say that…"

With a wry chuckle, I started the car and set off.

First up, I went to the supermarket closest to the dorm. There were too many zombies there to count, and they all came rushing toward me, reacting to the sound of the car engine.

I hit the brakes in a panic. Even I might be in danger if that huge horde of zombies surrounded me on all sides and bit me everywhere, so I parked a little ways away and went into a dark alley. There, I waited for zombies to approach me, and one by one, I tied them up and laid them down on the ground.

Once I eventually finished clearing the area near where I'd parked the car, I went into the supermarket. I lured all the zombies inside to the entrance, then repeated the process.

Halfway through, I ran out of rope, and with no other option, I looked for a replacement down the aisles swarming with zombies. Fortunately, however, the shop was half supermarket, half hardware store, so I found a huge range of rope in the materials section.

I kept going for quite a while after that, and in the end, I tied up more than fifty zombies, leaving me completely exhausted. Still, I didn't feel comfortable having them lying all over the place, so one at a time, I dragged the zombies by their feet to the stockroom.

By the time I'd finished securing the store, it was a little after one PM. I had to hurry up and gather supplies to take back to the dorm. I began putting packs of sushi and steaks with the nearest expiration dates in my shopping basket, since it would only go bad if I left it here. I also helped myself to some vegetables including green onions and cabbage.

The shopping basket was soon full, so I returned to the car, moved it in front of the entrance, and loaded up the goods. It was so much fun taking stuff from the supermarket without worrying about the prices. I'd thought that what Haruka said earlier had seemed pretty inappropriate, but maybe I was the one who'd been wrong; I *was* basically looting this place. I was only doing it to survive, though, so I hoped the people who owned the store would forgive me.

I took a break at one point and ate the omelet that Haruka had made for me to restore my strength. After lunch, I went back to work—and by the time I was done, the passenger seat, back seat, and the trunk of the car were filled with five shopping baskets packed to the brim with food.

It was a relief to see that we'd hardly made a dent in the store, even with our haul. There was also a considerable supply of canned goods and freeze-dried foods, so it looked like we wouldn't have to worry about starving for a while. That said, there was no guarantee that we'd be able to take everything in the supermarket, of course, since other survivors might also come here.

On my way out, I came up with the idea of putting a sign on the door. I tore a sheet of paper from a notebook in the stationery section, scribbled a message saying that the five of us were taking shelter in the dormitory of a girls' high school, and taped it to the automatic doors of the supermarket. Maybe now we'd be able to contact other survivors.

Driving carefully the whole way, I returned to the girls' dorm to see Haruka and Tsukishiro standing guard outside. They ran toward me as I arrived and opened up the gate.

"Kousaka!! I'm so glad you're safe…!!" Tsukishiro exclaimed emotionally.

"I told you, didn't I?" Haruka said, proudly puffing out her chest. "Yuuma's the strongest, so there's nothing to worry about."

The way Tsukishiro saw it, going out to get provisions was a quest that forced you to put your life on the line. It might've been best to make it look like I'd had a harder time of it, so she didn't get suspicious of me being a zombie…

"It's just as Haruka says: I'm the strongest, so you can leave supply gathering to me," I said confidently, deciding what we needed most right now was a sense of security.

Tsukishiro blushed and looked away. "…No. Now's not the time for feelings like that…" It was too quiet for me to make out, though, so I was left wondering what she'd been mumbling about.

Haruka, on the other hand, was glaring at me.

"Are you trying to come off as the big, strong protector type? Trying to get Tsukishiro to like you?"

"Hey, all I did was agree with what you said."

"*Hmph…* I feel like a *real* man would act humble in a situation like that."

"Well, sorry." It seemed like Haruka hadn't realized my true intentions in saying what I had. "Anyway, let's start unloading the goods."

Haruka and Tsukishiro cried out with joy when I opened the trunk.

"Wow, look at all this stuff! You're ruthless, stealing so much!"

"Is that a compliment...?"

"Kousaka, I'm sorry we have to depend on you like this, but it looks like we won't have to stress about food for a while."

"Don't worry about it. I also brought snacks, so feel free to take whatever you like."

"Trust Yuuma to know what we really need!" Delighted, Haruka was about to jump in when Tsukishiro stopped her.

"Hyuuga, please wait for just a moment. First, I want to make a record of how many items we've taken and from which store."

"—Huh? You want to do that for every single item in these five baskets?"

"Of course. We have to pay for it if we happen to meet someone who works for the store."

"Uh, that'll be tough to do. Considering what's happened to the world, don't you think we should be able to just go ahead and take what we need?"

"It's the only way to stop myself from feeling guilty. Please," Tsukishiro added with a bow.

"You sure take things seriously, don't you, Tsukishiro?" I blurted out.

"People often laugh at me for being so serious, but that's just how I am."

"Oh, I wasn't criticizing you—I'm impressed. I never would've even thought of making a record of what I've taken. I think it's such a wonderful, kind idea."

"Y-you do...?"

Tsukishiro smiled shyly, then her expression turned serious

again. "Kousaka," she said, giving me an even deeper bow. "On behalf of everyone in the dorm, thank you from the bottom of our hearts for going out to procure us food. And once again...I apologize for my earlier rudeness."

"You don't have to bow to me. I don't mind at all, and besides, we're going to continue working together to stay alive."

"Thank you... Let us take care of these supplies you brought back, so you just take some time to relax."

At Tsukishiro's suggestion, I went off to take a bath and got myself all nice and clean. Even though I was alone, I felt weirdly tense bathing in the large tub of a girls' dorm.

When I left the bathroom about twenty minutes later, I saw that Haruka and Tsukishiro had finished making a list of the items I'd brought back. We were going to eat the food that wouldn't stay fresh for very long first, so we laid out packs of sashimi and sushi on the table.

"Honestly, up until this morning, I had thought it wouldn't be long before we starved to death. But thanks to you, Kousaka, I've started to see a future where we stay alive. However, if we're going to do that, we all need to work together," Tsukishiro said, her voice filled with a quiet resolve. "I've only had minimal interaction with Hoshimiya and Ichinose up to now, but that will have to change. We'll also need to set up rules for communal living."

With that, Tsukishiro went upstairs to bring the other two girls down for dinner. I was really glad I'd been able to give Tsukishiro some hope for survival.

Ichinose followed Tsukishiro into the cafeteria, and her eyes widened in surprise.

"—Wow...!! This is amazing... It feels like we're celebrating someone's birthday...!!"

"What?! Kousaka, did you bring all this here?!" Hoshimiya exclaimed, a few paces behind Ichinose. "When you said you were going out to get food for us, I thought it'd just be mountains of canned goods...!! Weren't there any zombies there?"

"Maybe around fifty of them. I tied them all up and locked them up in the storage area."

"For real?! They didn't bite you?!"

"I managed to evade their attacks pretty easily."

"That's crazy! Are you a martial arts expert or something?"

"No, nothing like that. I don't play sports, either, so my stamina's pretty bad. It really wore me out."

"O-oh yeah? I don't know how you did it, but what I do know is that you worked your butt off!" Hoshimiya said, full of admiration. All of a sudden, she seemed to get some sort of idea, because Hoshimiya smiled wickedly and sat down on my right.

She pulled her chair over so we were sitting close together, then looked up at me through her eyelashes. I could almost feel my eyes gravitating toward the ample cleavage shown off by her camisole.

"Seeing as you worked so hard, why don't I feed you your sushi? What do you want to start with?"

"Wha—?! No, I'm—"

Just then, Haruka sat down with a *thud* in the chair facing me, making her presence known. No need for that—of course I was going to refuse Hoshimiya's offer...

"It's okay; I can manage on my own."

But Hoshimiya kept persisting. "Please, I insist. Think of it as my way of thanking you for saving our lives."

"W-well, uh..."

It was hard to say no when she put it like that. And besides, if we were going to be living here together from now on, I had to stop being so stubborn.

"All right, then…"

"Welcome! Table for one? What will it be, sir?"

"Um, I'd like the rosy seabass…"

"Rosy seabass coming right up!" Hoshimiya said in a singsongy voice.

She picked up a pair of chopsticks and lifted a piece of sushi to my mouth.

"Say *aah*."

"…Thank you."

"Hee-hee! Is it good?"

"Uh-huh…"

"I'm so glad! It's not like I made it, though."

"Ha-ha-ha-ha-ha…" I laughed dryly and fearfully turned my gaze across the table.

Haruka gave me a cold smile, and when our eyes met, she stomped on my foot and began grinding it under the table.

How could I possibly enjoy the taste of sushi under the circumstances?

Even Hoshimiya seemed to notice the change in atmosphere around us, and she tilted her head slightly when she saw Haruka frowning.

"What's wrong, Hyuuga? You look so scary. Did you want a piece of rosy seabass, too?"

"Something like that."

"You don't have to look so upset. There's plenty more."

"I guess I'm just the sort of person who wants to keep the things I like all for myself."

"Oh, don't be a baby. We all have to share, since we're living under the same roof."

"...*Right. Sorry for being so immature.*"

The way she said that made all the hair on my body stand on end. Then she stabbed the top of my foot with all ten of her toenails.

It didn't hurt, but I thought it best to retreat.

"Sorry, I have to use the men's room."

I got up and headed to the bathroom, deciding to lock myself in there until all this blew over. However, I quickly changed my mind and left, not wanting everyone to think I was pooing.

Ichinose was waiting for me in the hallway. Now that I thought about it, they only had girls' bathrooms in the building.

"Oh! Sorry," I apologized reflexively. I went to walk away when she grabbed the hem of my shirt.

"—Huh?"

"...Maybe you should wrap a magazine around your arm."

"...Excuse me?"

"When you're fighting zombies, the greatest risk is probably having it bite you on the forearm. So I thought it might help to wrap magazines around your arms and fix them in place with sticky tape...," she muttered hesitantly, keeping an eye on my reaction.

"...Ah. I thought it'd be good if I could find some gauntlets, but you're right. I could probably use magazines the same way."

Not that I needed it, but it might come in handy when I took Haruka outside.

"Thanks for the great idea. I saw some magazines when I was looking around the dorm earlier, so I'll try it out as soon as possible!"

"Hee-hee-hee..."

Ichinose gave a satisfied smiled as I thanked her. Then she headed back to the cafeteria without going to the bathroom. Had she just been waiting here to tell me her idea...?

I returned to the cafeteria, where Hoshimiya began feeding me sushi again and Haruka continued to attack my feet. By the time I'd finished dinner, I barely had any recollection of what I'd eaten.

As we cleared the table, I saw Tsukishiro wash out the sushi packaging and separate it from the general trash, though I doubted anyone was still around to recycle plastics...

Once everything on the table was put away, the five of us sat down again. Tsukishiro stood up, looked each of us in the eye, then opened her mouth to speak.

"As of today, the five of us will be living together. I expect we'll be faced with all manner of hardships, but let's work together to make it through them. Next, let's all give a brief self-introduction. I'm Mai Tsukishiro, a third-year student. I was in the Japanese archery club, so I know how to handle a bow and arrow."

"Yeah! That's our leader!" Hoshimiya shouted. She seemed to be in high spirits now that she knew we had a way of getting food.

"Let's go clockwise around the table. Stand up when you introduce yourself, okay? Hoshimiya, your turn."

"Okay. Um, I'm Lisa Hoshimiya. I like playing video games... Unlike Tsukishiro, I don't have any skills that might be useful to everyone, but I'm happy to take care of any chores!"

"I'm Yuuma Kousaka. My special skill is...tying up zombies, I guess. You can let me take care of gathering supplies, and feel free to let me know if there's anything you want in particular."

"I'm Haruka Hyuuga. I don't have any useful skills, but I do have an…*interesting* video of Yuuma, so if anyone wants to see it—"

"Don't you dare."

"Aw, now I'm curious. What's it of?"

"Hee-hee! I'll show it to you when we have a chance, Hoshimiya." A meaningful smile crossed Haruka's face.

I wondered when they might have that *chance* she'd mentioned…

"Okay, last but not least, Ichinose, introduce yourself."

Prompted by Tsukishiro, Ichinose stood up. Her expression was taut with nerves.

"…Um, I'm Ayumi Ichinose. I, uh… I don't have any skills in particular… But I like to read. I can read manuals or instructions for you if you don't feel like doing it yourself. I'm a science student, so I often read technical books and other publications…and I can also do simple mechanical repairs."

"Oh wow! That's a huge help!" Hoshimiya cheered with joy. I felt the same way.

"We'll have to fix anything that breaks down ourselves from here on out. It's a good thing we have you," I told Ichinose.

"Hee-hee-hee…" She laughed shyly, then quietly sat down.

Once we'd all introduced ourselves, Tsukishiro got to her feet again. "Let's take the rest of the day to relax. We don't have any work to do inside the dorm right now, so feel free to do whatever you want until tonight."

"So is it okay if I take a shower…?"

"Sure."

"Yaaay!!" Hoshimiya cheered again and jumped up from her chair.

Meanwhile, Ichinose covered her mouth and yawned.

"I think I'll go to my room and rest… I've been so worried lately that I haven't been able to sleep…"

"I'll come and wake you up when it's time for dinner."

"Thanks…"

With that, we called an end to our lunchtime meeting and everyone stood up to go. Hoshimiya immediately approached me.

"Kousaka, do you have any plans now? How about playing a game with me? After I take a shower, that is."

"Sorry, I'm going back to the supermarket. With Haruka, this time."

"Oh, you are…? Okay, take care." Hoshimiya sounded a little disappointed as she left the cafeteria. Maybe there was something she'd wanted to talk about…

"I had a feeling this would happen. You've become super popular with everyone."

I hadn't realized Haruka was standing right next to me, and she gave me a searching look.

"I'm not *super popular*. They're all just grateful for my help."

"Are you an idiot? A girl doesn't wear revealing clothes like that when she eats sushi if she's only feeling *grateful*."

"I don't know what eating sushi's got to do with it, but you can't assume that from how much skin a person's showing. Hoshimiya just seems to like those sorts of clothes."

"You're a lost cause, Yuuma. Never in my life have I met someone as stupid as you."

"That's an awful thing to say…"

"…Still, I was glad you prioritized your plans with me when Hoshimiya invited you to play games with her…," Haruka said with a shy smile.

As we stood there talking, Tsukishiro approached us.

"I'd like to assign rooms to the two of you. Let me know if you have any preferences, like which floor you want to be on or if you want a corner room."

"I'd like to be on the first floor," I said. "I want to be able to respond right away if a zombie comes climbing over the fence."

"Thank you for thinking about security. Okay then, I'll clean out the room closest to the entrance for you. How about you, Hyuuga?"

"Whatever Yuuma wants is fine."

"……? Do you mean you'd like a room next to him?"

"Huh? Aren't we sharing the same room?" Haruka asked, cocking her head.

Tsukishiro looked at me in surprise, but it was my first time hearing this as well, and I didn't know how to react.

"Boys aren't allowed in the dorm, but Yuuma's going to be living here because I insisted. I'll share a room with him and keep an eye out to make sure he doesn't cause any problems."

"That's not necessary. I've already determined Kousaka to be trustworthy, so please sleep in different rooms."

"I know he may not look it, but Yuuma's a predator. I mean, only yesterday, he—"

"Don't say something that might alarm her!" I said, stopping Haruka before she could say anything incriminating. I didn't know what she'd been about to say, but I could think of too many possibilities, like squeezing her breasts by the river and gazing at her naked body through the frosted glass.

Arguing with her was likely to cause problems, though, so I just decided to do what she said.

"I'm fine sharing a room with Haruka. And if something does happen, I'll have her as my alibi to prove I'm not the culprit."

"Still, don't you think it's problematic for a man and a woman who aren't married to sleep in the same room? And if you really are a predator, isn't there a risk you'll take advantage of Hyuuga?"

"...I don't mind, as long as he's willing to take responsibility...," Hyuuga mumbled embarrassedly. Though I really wished she'd deny that I might take advantage of her... "We've known each other since grade school, so I think I'll be able to keep him under control. Please let us share a room so I can keep an eye on him."

I couldn't believe how rude some of the things Haruka was saying were, but I knew that if I made any sort of protest, we'd just end up getting tangled in the weeds. So I decided to shut my mouth for now.

"...Really? Since grade school...?" Tsukishiro muttered to herself. Was it just my imagination, or did she look a little sad?

However, she quickly went back to serious mode.

"All right. Then the two of you can use the room closest to the entrance. And since I'm now the dorm manager here, I need to be able to respond immediately should something happen, so I'll move into the room next to yours. I'll come running if I hear anything unusual."

With that settled, we moved into the dorm. Each room had a bunk bed, desks, and chests of drawers, so we didn't have to furnish them ourselves.

First, we moved everything left behind by the previous resident into an unused room. I let Haruka take care of all the stuff in the drawers that I was better off not seeing, while I changed the bedsheets and pillowcases.

We were finished in under half an hour.

"We're all set with our new home!" Haruka said proudly,

looking around the room. I felt my heart skip a beat—she was talking like this was our first night as a married couple…

"Yuuma, do you want top or bottom bunk?"

"You can choose."

"Then I'm taking the top one. I've never slept in a bunk bed! ♪"

Haruka excitedly climbed the ladder up to the top bunk. I'd see up her skirt if she kept going like that, but I didn't look away because I knew she was wearing leggings. Even if I couldn't see her panties, men still fantasized about being able to see up a girl's skirt—

But for some reason, she wasn't wearing her leggings, and I caught a glimpse of her light blue panties at the top of those milky-white thighs.

Flustered, I quickly turned away.

"Yuuma! I'm so high up!" Haruka rolled over on the top bunk and waved.

"Y-yeah."

"…? What's wrong?"

"No, it's nothing."

"Something's clearly wrong; I can see it all over your face. What happened? All I did was climb up the ladder—"

Haruka seemed to have figured out the reason behind my strange reaction. She pressed her skirt down and, with an embarrassed looked, asked, "Yuuma… Did you look…?"

"…Sorry."

"Geez… I can't even let my guard down for a second…"

"No, it's not like that. I thought you were wearing leggings…"

"I took them off because it was hot. I figured we wouldn't be climbing over any more fences today."

"Climbing a ladder without wearing leggings is way too careless."

"I trusted you."

"…I feel so bad, hearing you say that."

"If anything, don't you think it's *more* perverted trying to look up my skirt at my leggings than trying to see my underwear?"

"I don't know how to answer that…"

"Honestly… You're so obsessed with me…"

"Why do you look happy about that?"

"Don't try to make it sound like this is my fault. I'm really angry at you right now. You're going to have to make up for this—"

Just then, someone knocked at the door.

"Have you two finished moving in?" Tsukishiro called out. She'd come to check on us, and I told her we had.

"Good… By the way, I could hear the two of you arguing from the hallway. Perhaps it would be better for you to take separate rooms after all?"

…Apparently, the walls here weren't all that thick. I was embarrassed that Tsukishiro had heard about what I'd done.

"We're fine. That's just our way of communicating, isn't it, Yuuma?"

"Y-yeah."

I didn't know whether it was a good idea to call peeking up Haruka's skirt *communicating*, but I thought it best to go along with whatever she said.

"I see… In that case, I'll stop meddling," Tsukishiro replied, the disapproval evident in her eyes. It looked like she was stopping herself from voicing what she really wanted to say…

"Anyway, Kousaka, I wanted to ask you to guard the gate, if you wouldn't mind."

"You want *me* to guard the gate?"

"Could you keep an eye out for any survivors and make sure no zombies climb over the fence? I haven't slept since yesterday, so I'd like to take a short rest."

"What…?! Don't tell me you've been watching the gate ever since the zombies first showed up yesterday…?"

"That's correct."

"Without any sleep…?"

"Naturally."

…Now that I thought about it, Tsukishiro was always looking out the window, even when we were eating…

"Couldn't you have asked Hoshimiya or Ichinose to take over for you…?"

"I haven't told those two about guard duty. Pretty much the only weapons we have in the dorm are a bow and arrow and kitchen knives, so I figured I was the only one who would be able to handle intruders safely from a distance."

"…I understand. Okay, I'll take over guard duty now, so make sure you get plenty of rest. And when I go out tomorrow, I'll see if I can find a weapon that's easy for a girl to use."

So—sadly my outing with Haruka was postponed until the next day.

I could handle guard duty alone, but Haruka wanted to do it with me, so the two of us stood watch at the entrance to the dorm. We scanned our surroundings through the black iron fence that encircled the building.

"Hey, Yuuma," Haruka said, playing with the bow and arrow she'd borrowed from Tsukishiro. "I know it's a little late to ask this now, but aren't you going to tell the others that you can turn yourself into a zombie?"

"No. And I don't want you to tell them about it, either. Everyone might go crazy."

"Go crazy? Over you, you mean? You're already popular."

"No, if anything, it'd be the opposite. Normal people don't want to live with zombies, so there's a chance they'd kick us out."

"But you're completely safe to be around."

"We don't know that for sure. It's only been about twenty-four hours since I became a zombie. And even if I really am safe to be around, there aren't many people who'd just take my word for that. Most people would probably assume I'd suddenly become like all the other zombies and attack them."

"You think so? Tsukishiro and the others here are all friendly toward you, so why don't you try explaining the situation to them and come up with a plan for what to do if they reject you?"

"The girls who are with us right now might accept me, but we have no idea how other people who come to live here might react."

"Oh yeah… If another guy came to live here, he might get jealous of how popular you are and start trying to find fault with you. But even he would be in trouble if you left and we stopped getting supplies."

"Sometimes, people act on emotion instead of logic. There are bound to be people who would refuse to live with a zombie, even if they had no other way of getting food with me gone."

"I still think most people would say they wanted to work with you."

"Even if we put it to a vote and the majority lets me stay here, some people might still refuse to live with me and move out, and I wouldn't be able to protect them."

"Ah. So it isn't really about you. It's more for the sake of protecting the community, right? The way I see it, if the people here *do* reject us, all we have to do is find another place to stay."

"True, things would be easier if we lived only with people who'd cooperate with us. But thinking about the future, I want to live with as big a group as possible. We need as many people with different skills as we can get—people with knowledge about medicine, machines, and agriculture."

"I see... You've thought a lot about this... Okay, I understand. Your little secret will be our little secret. Hee-hee!"

"What's so funny?"

"It's kind of fun keeping it just between the two of us." Haruka smiled like a naughty child.

She was right; it didn't sound all that bad.

After that, we chatted about all sorts of random things as we continued to watch the gate. Every now and then, we'd see a zombie in the distance. Even though they wouldn't come near us if we didn't do anything, we tied them all up and laid them down on the ground, thinking about the future.

About half an hour went by.

"...I'm bored," Haruka murmured, stifling a yawn. "Isn't anything exciting going to happen?"

"Don't say something inappropriate like that."

"But I'm booored."

"You can always go back to the room if you want."

"There's no internet, so there's nothing to do there."

"That's true..."

"I know this isn't something I should be thinking two days after a zombie outbreak, but I wish I had something to help me pass the time."

"Everything's free, so why don't you bring back whatever you want when we go out tomorrow?"

"I'll do that. Let's see, what do I want...? Something that'll come in handy in the future, huh? Maybe I'll pick up some boxercise gear to train with."

"Don't forget: Close combat against zombies is dangerous."

"Then maybe I'll get a bow and arrow. I can get a bunch of them, in fact, and Tsukishiro can show us all how to use them." Haruka placed the arrow against the bowstring and pulled it back lightly. "But according to the movies, you have to hit a zombie directly through the brain to take them down, right?"

"Yeah. I don't know if the zombies in our world are the same, but you won't be able to become an expert at using a bow and arrow overnight."

"In that case...should I get a baseball bat and do some practice swings?"

"That sounds good, but would you actually enjoy it?"

"Not sure. Training is important, but I also want time to play games and read."

"Let's think about what we want to bring back by the time we leave tomorrow."

"You got it. Hmm... We could also look for games to play together so we can get to know everyone better."

"Good idea."

"What kind of games should we look for? Maybe we should ask the others to fill out a questionnaire during dinner. Anyway, Yuuma, do you feel like afternoon tea?"

"That was a sudden change in subject."

"I was just thinking it's almost four."

"I'm fine, but you can go inside and grab a bite to eat in the cafeteria."

"No, not like that. I was talking about having afternoon tea out here."

"What, like a picnic?"

"Sort of. The dorm has furniture everywhere, so I'm sure no one would mind if we moved a table and a few chairs out here. I always dreamed of having afternoon tea outdoors, but my parents never let me; they always said the chairs would get dirty."

"I don't see why not. It'd be handy to have chairs out here for when we're on guard duty."

"Yay! So go and get them for us!"

"Who, me?"

"Sure. I'll grab the tea and sweets."

"That'd leave no one here to stand guard."

"Oh right. But it should be okay if it's just for a little while. I mean, you already tied up all the zombies in the area."

"We can't do that. Here, I'll go get the table, then go back for the tea and sweets."

"But if you're not here, I won't be able to deal with an emergency if something actually happens... Fine, I'll get everything ready," Haruka declared, then began moving furniture out of the dorm.

She carried out a round wooden table without much trouble, and I realized she was actually pretty strong. "Hup. There we go." Then she brought two chairs and set them up next to the entrance, and we were all set to begin our elegant afternoon tea.

I was amazed by her creativity and can-do attitude to enjoy a world in an apocalypse.

"By the way, shouldn't we invite the others?"

"I think Tsukishiro and Ichinose are still sleeping, and Hoshimiya seems to be taking a bath. We'd only be bothering them with an invitation."

"I guess you have a point."

"We have to set up some ground rules for living in the dorm, like when it's okay to talk to someone when they're in their room."

"Yeah, definitely. Maybe we should have people put up a Do NOT DISTURB sign outside their door when they're sleeping... That said, it's a pain in the ass having to go to the fifth floor every time we want to call them downstairs."

"Should we ask Hoshimiya and Ichinose to move to the ground floor?"

"Yeah, probably. For the dorm rules, we also need to figure out how to make it more efficient to use the one bath we have for both men and women."

"It would be annoying having separate times for each gender; it's better if everyone can use it whenever they want. We could make a sign that says MEN on the front and WOMEN on the back—and hang it on the door while we're using the bath."

"We'd still need to have some sort of idea who's using the bath at what time, though, otherwise we'll just end up—"

"Aaaaahh!!"

All of a sudden, we heard a scream from the direction of the bath. It sounded like Hoshimiya.

"Aaahh! Nooo!"

Hoshimiya kept screaming, the panic clear in her voice. She must be in trouble over there.

Had a zombie somehow managed to get in?!

"Yuuma!"

"Haruka, wait here!"

I ran inside the building without taking off my shoes and came to a stop in front of the changing area for the bath.

What if it wasn't a zombie that Hoshimiya had encountered, but just a large bug or something? I hadn't heard the sound of a window breaking... Still, if it was a zombie attacking her, Hoshimiya's life might be in danger.

I braced myself, opened the door to the changing room, and ran into the bathroom. Hoshimiya was covered in a bright-red liquid from the neck down, trying to wipe it off. I was shocked; that looked like zombie blood.

A few seconds later, I smelled a telltale putrid odor. But I couldn't find the attacker.

"Are you all right? Where's the zombie?"

"—Aaahh!!"

Hoshimiya covered her chest with her hands and squatted down. It wasn't wrong for a girl to react like that in this sort of situation, but we had bigger issues right now.

"Tell me where the zombie is!!"

"...It's not that. The water coming out of the shower just suddenly went all weird...," she said, pointing to the detachable showerhead on the floor. The floor was stained bright red around it.

I turned the showerhead toward the wall and ran the hot water. What came out instead was polluted water, reeking of decay.

"It may contain the zombie virus! You have to wash it off quickly!"

But turning on all the other showers only released more nasty-smelling hot water.

"Oh! Get in the bath!" I said, and Hoshimiya dived in the bathtub.

The zombie blood clinging to her body dissolved in the hot water, but we couldn't let ourselves relax just yet.

"The virus might still be alive, so hurry and get out of the wat—"

That was when I noticed Hoshimiya looking uncomfortable.

"Um… I will, so could you turn around…?"

"S-sorry!"

I took my eyes off Hoshimiya's naked body submerged in the clear, hot water and hurriedly turned away. Then I heard her step out of the tub.

This was a big problem for a lot of reasons… As I stepped out into the changing area, I started to run through in my mind what we'd have to do.

While Hoshimiya got dressed, I got my other dorm mates together in the cafeteria and warned them not to use the tap water because it might be contaminated.

"I checked the other taps in the dorm, and contaminated water came out of all of them. A zombie may have gotten into the water pipes somewhere."

This meant it wasn't just food we needed to stock up on, but drinking water as well.

"I'm sorry, Tsukishiro, but I need you to guard the gate. Haruka, Ichinose, could you both secure all the taps in the dormitory with rope so no one accidentally uses the water? Also…Hoshimiya and I are going to move to the fifth floor. You should avoid getting too close to us until I tell you it's safe."

"You're moving to the fifth floor? What for?"

"…Hoshimiya was covered in contaminated water. We need to monitor her progress to see if she was infected with the virus."

"Oh…" The gravity of the situation seemed to have finally sunk in for Haruka.

There was a chance we might lose one of our dorm mates.

Hoshimiya eventually showed up wearing a T-shirt, so we grabbed some food and drinks and went to her room.

"...I wonder if I'll really turn into a zombie...," she mumbled once we were alone.

"I don't know... Did the contaminated water get in your mouth?"

"I don't think so. I was washing off and noticed the smell right away."

"Then the virus probably didn't enter your body, and you should be okay..."

We still didn't know if it really was a virus turning people into zombies. If it was, though, I'd heard that they could even get into you through your eyes, so we had to be extremely vigilant.

"How long do I have to wait to see whether I'll turn into a zombie?"

"At least an hour, I'd say. Still, if possible, I want to keep an eye on you for at least half a day."

"Until tomorrow morning...? Will you stay with me in my room tonight?"

"As long as you don't mind."

"Not at all. Besides, you'd probably worry if you didn't keep watch over someone at risk, right?"

"Yeah... The dorm rooms can't be locked from the outside, so the only way to prevent other people from getting hurt would be for me to keep an eye on you—or to tie up your hands and feet."

"That'd suck, being tied up for half a day..."

"You can do whatever you want, though, since I'll be watching you."

"Thanks," she said quietly with a sigh. "Honestly, it doesn't even seem real to me that I could become a zombie. I know the world's a mess right now, but I still can't believe it."

"I know how you feel. I still wonder whether everything that's happened since yesterday might all be a dream."

"I wish it was. You saw me naked."

"I…"

"Did my body look weird?"

"How should I know? I didn't look that closely."

"Liar. You were staring at me after I got into the bathtub."

"I was just watching to make sure you got all the zombie blood off… Though, your body did enter my field of vision…"

"You got a good look at my boobs, didn't you?"

"…I think I might've caught a glimpse."

"So what'd you think? I'm pretty proud of their shape."

"I wasn't looking at you like that because I was in anti-zombie mode at the time. I was so focused on the blood that I barely remember anything else."

"Hmm, is that right…? Then did you see my tummy? I've gained a bit of weight recently, so I must look all gross."

"Huh? It looked pretty flat to me."

"So you do remember."

"Uh…"

After catching me out, Hoshimiya gave a shy smile. Her face was bright red.

"Now…this is a very important question… Did you see below my belly button?"

"…Um…"

"Wait, forget it. I don't want to know." She cut me off and covered her ears. "That won't change anything now— Let's drop the subject," Hoshimiya said with a clap, before continuing at her usual rapid pace.

"Like, I could turn into a zombie, and *this* is what we're talking about? Having you see me naked is a major incident, but I might not even be able to have a regular conversation with you in a few minutes, so I need to make sure I don't have any regrets... That said, how should I be spending what could be my final moments...?"

"I don't know... It'd be nice if you could talk to your family one last time, but phones aren't working..."

"If you meet them after I turn into a zombie, could you thank them for everything they did for me?"

"Sure."

"—Ha-ha! That sounded like something a person who's about to die might say in a movie," she said, poking fun at herself. But I didn't feel like laughing.

"I always thought it was a corny line, but after what's happened, I get it," Hoshimiya continued. "You want people to think of you as a good person after you die, and you want to leave them a nice message."

"I get what you mean."

"*Haah*... When I think about the fact that my life might end today, all sorts of regrets come bubbling to the surface. I should have done more than just play games."

"Like what, for example? If there's anything we can do in here, I'll help you out."

"Let's see... For one, I wish I'd gotten myself a boyfriend and done all sorts of fun things with him... Honestly, I'm just one big raging ball of desire, aren't I?"

"No, I know how you feel. If a zombie bit me, I'd probably think the same way."

It was like I was watching myself from the day before, and I found myself more than a little surprised that girls thought like that, too.

"You do, do you…?"

Hoshimiya thought that over for a moment, then for some reason, she suddenly covered her face with both hands, hiding everything from her eyes down.

"…Then how about having sex with me?"

"Wha—?!"

"You said that if there was anything we could do in this room, you'd help me out," Hoshimiya pressed, shyly yet surely.

I couldn't help looking at her ample breasts.

"I—I did say, but…"

"Do you have a girlfriend, Kousaka?"

"No…"

"Then what's the problem? Or…don't you want to have sex with me?"

"That's not the issue…"

"Stop beating around the bush… Didn't you get excited when you saw me naked…?"

"Well… It was an emergency, so I wasn't thinking about it at the time. But I guess…"

"Glad to see you being honest with yourself."

The corner of her eyes crinkled in a smile. Even her ears and hands were bright red now.

"…There's just one problem if we do that."

"Hmm? What is it?"

"We don't know exactly how the zombie virus infects people. Bites might not be the only way it spreads; it's possible that it could be transmitted through the mucous membrane."

"What does that mean?"

"Like through kissing…or sex stuff."

"Oh right. So if I have the zombie virus in my body, I'll end up infecting you."

"Exactly."

Of course this was all just a ruse; I'd already contracted the zombie virus, so it wouldn't matter for me if we did anything like that, regardless of whether Hoshimiya was infected.

But if she wasn't, then *I* might infect *her*.

"So I feel really bad about it, but I'll have to turn you down this time…"

"Okay… I understand. Forget what I just said."

Hoshimiya turned her back to me, and a heavy silence filled the room.

But after about three minutes, she suddenly turned back around to face me.

"I'm seriously regretting suggesting something so embarrassing."

"L-let's just forget about it. Anyone can make mistakes, especially when they're facing the possibility of imminent death."

I should know: It had happened to me.

"I don't want you thinking I'm a slut, though," Hoshimiya said. "I'm in a life-or-death situation…and I just thought I wouldn't mind doing it with you."

"…I'm honored."

"Don't think I'll say yes if you come begging for sex after I turn out to be okay. You only get the one chance."

"I won't."

"You're sure? I know you were staring at my breasts when we first met."

"That…was just my natural instincts…"

"Would you have said yes if I'd tried to seduce you wearing a camisole?"

"...Of course not."

"What was that weird pause, then?"

"What pause?" I tried to bluff, but Hoshimiya just gave me a weak smile.

"...Hey, can we just chat for a little while? ...It's kinda scary when things are quiet."

"Sure."

"Then, do you mind if I call you by your first name, Yuuma?"

"Not at all."

"You can call me Lisa."

"Okay."

"Great. So...what should we talk about...? Yuuma... Don't you get scared fighting zombies?"

"I mean...of course I do." I thought back to how I'd felt before I discovered I wouldn't lose my self-awareness after turning into a zombie. "Getting bitten by a zombie is pretty much a death sentence that turns you into a monster like the ones we see— Sorry. I shouldn't say that when there's a chance it might happen to you."

"No, it's okay... You're right; it's terrifying to think about... Yet all I did while you were out getting supplies was laze around in my room... If I don't turn, I'll need to help everyone out more...!!" she said, clasping her hands tightly.

I continued talking with Lisa, feeling guilty the whole time that I was lying to her...

# DAY 3

I kept watch of Lisa's progress throughout the night, not sleeping a wink, but by the next morning, she still seemed as human as ever.

It was six AM. More than twelve hours had passed since she'd been exposed to the contaminated water, so it was probably safe to assume she was fine. I didn't know if the virus hadn't been in the tap water, if it was and just hadn't gotten into her body, or if the only way to get infected was directly from a bite… But whatever the reason, one thing was clear: We could no longer use the tap water.

Lisa and I went downstairs to the cafeteria and told the other three that she was okay, which was a relief to everyone.

"Thank you so much, Kousaka," Tsukishiro said, bowing deeply. "…I hate to ask this when I know you must be tired, but I was hoping you might be able to go out and get us water somewhere…"

"Of course."

What I really wanted to do was sleep, but the dorm only had soft drinks, so our health might be affected if I didn't go out to get water soon.

"I had considered the possibility that we might not be able to use the tap water at some point, but I didn't think it would happen so soon…," Tsukishiro continued with a sigh. "I'm afraid we'll need to ask you to find drinking water for us now, as well as food. Will you be okay doing that?"

"No problem. Leave it to me."

"Thank you… There's a limited supply of water at stores, though, so we'll need to use it sparingly. Assuming we use the contaminated water to flush the toilet, we can no longer fill the bath, so we won't be able to wash ourselves every day. We'll also have to think about how to do laundry…"

I could feel the atmosphere in the cafeteria grow heavier as we went over our current situation. There was a limit to how far I could venture out to find supplies, so we might have to move somewhere else once we used up all the water at nearby stores. I decided to keep an eye out for buildings that looked safe when I went out…

"Well then, I'll head off to get supplies."

"Okay, Yuuma! It's dangerous if you fall asleep behind the wheel, so I'll drive you!" Haruka said brightly. She took the car keys and stepped outside. I decided not to argue, since I had promised to take her to the supermarket.

Lisa caught me just as I was leaving the dorm.

"I'm sorry, Yuuma. You didn't get any sleep because of me, and now you're going out to get water…"

"That's okay. Don't worry about me; you just go back inside and rest. I might ask you to watch the gate at some point."

"Okay. I'll see you later then."

Lisa gave me a small wave as I got into the passenger seat, and Haruka suddenly stepped on the accelerator—hard.

"…Yuuma. Did something happen with Hoshimiya last night?"

Her sudden question blew away all my drowsiness.

"No, nothing."

"Are you sure? The way you two called each other by your first names, you sounded awfully close…"

"Oh, that… She suggested it. That's all…"

"Hmm… But wouldn't a sex-crazed guy like you have all sorts of strange thoughts spending the night with Hoshimiya?"

"Of course not. We thought she was about to turn into a zombie."

"I see. And the two of you didn't find comfort in one another, thinking you might as well succumb to temptation if she was going to die soon?"

"O-of course not."

"What was that little stumble just now?"

"You must've imagined it."

All I'd done was think back to when Lisa propositioned me the night before, but Haruka still wasn't convinced.

"Something doesn't add up…"

"That's an unfair accusation. I might infect her with the virus if—and that's a big *if*—we did anything like that."

"Oh, that's true. I guess that means you can only sleep with another zombie."

"Guess so."

"Ah… I'm sorry I doubted you. So if you can only be intimate with another zombie, does that mean you see all female zombies as potential brides?"

"You're kidding, right?"

I couldn't say for sure, since I'd never seen a zombie naked, but I doubted that would get me excited…

"Never mind that," I told Haruka. "Stop yammering and focus on driving."

"You don't have to worry about that. Oh, by the way, do you remember when we went to the supermarket we're going to now, back in grade school?"

"...Sure."

"You don't, do you?"

"N-no, I do. We went there to buy sweets for Takuya's birthday party." I said it like I'd known it all along—but the truth was, I'd had to desperately dredge it up from my memories.

Haruka sounded delighted. "You do remember!"

"Of course. How could I forget? It feels like it was just yesterday."

"Then, question number one: What sweets and drinks did we buy that day?"

"Sorry, I can't remember those little details."

I immediately raised the white flag, and Haruka puffed out her cheeks in frustration.

"Yuuma, you forget way too much."

"Your memory's just too good."

"I don't see it like that. I'm not good at memorizing things, but I do tend to remember things that have to do with you."

"Did I really make that much of an impact on you when I was in grade school?"

"...That's not what I meant...," she mumbled, sounding embarrassed for some reason.

"Then why do you remember things involving me so well?"

"Stop talking to me. I'm going to focus on driving."

"What's with the one-eighty?!"

Haruka's gaze remained fixed on the road, so I didn't ask her any more questions.

After driving in silence for a while, we arrived at the supermarket I'd secured yesterday. There were zombies scattered around the parking lot that could still move around freely, and they came toward us when they heard the sound of the car engine. None of them looked familiar, so they must have come from somewhere else.

"Haruka, wait in the car. I'm going to tie them up. Leave the engine running, and step on the accelerator if anything happens."

I got out of the car with my rope at the ready and restrained the oncoming zombies one by one, lying them down where they were. Once the coast was clear, I went into the supermarket and looked around. None seemed to have made it inside.

I returned to the car, then brought Haruka back with me to the store.

"Hey, what did you do with the zombies that were inside the store yesterday?"

"I tied them all up and crowded them into the storage room."

"Can I go take a look?"

"It isn't a pretty sight, so I don't recommend it…"

"Just a quick peek?"

Haruka begged to see it, so I ended up leading her to the back of the store. The storage room was about the size of a convenience store, and it was filled with rows of incapacitated zombies.

"Wow!! This is amazing…!"

"Happy now…? Like I said, it isn't a pleasant sight…"

"Yeah. Okay then, let's get started with our shopping date."

"...Come again?"

"A *date*. We're all alone now, so let's do something couple-y," Haruka said in a voice that was almost a purr. *God, she's cute...*

However, I was rudely brought back to reality seeing the huge horde of zombies lying on the floor behind her.

"Don't tell me you can really enjoy shopping with all these zombies around..."

"Just don't let them enter your field of vision. We're all alone in a supermarket. Isn't that fun?"

"I—I guess...?"

I couldn't understand her way of thinking, but we started looking around. Haruka stopped in her tracks when we reached the pet section of the hardware side of the store; she was looking at a cage for a large dog. I figured she was thinking of using it for something. We could probably retrofit it into a sort of zombie trap—

"Yuuma, get inside for a sec."

"Why?!"

"I want to see you sitting in there. Is there any other reason I'd ask you to do that?"

"I was an idiot for asking."

"Ohh? Is my cute little doggy talking like a person again?"

"......"

"You haven't forgotten what you are, have you, Yuuma?"

"...*Woof.*"

"Very good. Now, in you go," Haruka said happily and pointed to the cage on display.

I knew by now that once Haruka set her mind on something, there was no changing it, so I moved the cage onto the floor and reluctantly went inside. Even though it was the biggest one they had, it was still pretty cramped...

"Good boy! Okay, I'm going to lock the door."

"Hey, don't do that!"

But there was no way to move around quickly in the narrow cage, and its door was mercilessly locked shut.

"Next, I'll take your photo. Yuuma, look this way."

"Like I care what you do anymore..."

"Really?! Then let's put a collar on you!"

"Sorry, I lied! I *do* care!"

"Too late now. The door won't unlock until you put a collar on and get your photo taken."

I was doomed...

"Can't you respect me as a human being?"

"Human...? Didn't you change jobs and become my dog the day before yesterday?"

"...*Hrnn.*"

That was how I ended up with a collar around my neck and Haruka taking pathetic photos of me.

"Yuuma, that collar really suits you. Do you want to wear it back to the dorm?"

"God, no. Please..."

Once Haruka was satisfied, I was allowed to take off the collar, and we walked over to the supermarket section to get drinking water. We started clearing out all the bottled water and tea into our shopping baskets and carried them to the car.

"This is pretty tough work... I reckon you could do this to lose weight…," Haruka said, already worn-out. I couldn't really blame her, though, since each basket weighed twelve kilograms filled with six two-liter bottles.

"Weren't you excited to go on a 'stealing spree in a deserted supermarket' yesterday?"

"I thought it'd just be a fancy food free-for-all. I didn't expect to have to carry bottle after bottle of water…"

"I've heard that humans drink more than two liters of water a day."

"That's ten liters for five people…and it isn't just drinking water we need, is it?"

"Pretty soon, we'll have to start going to other supermarkets for water."

"Maybe we should check the pockets of the zombies you tied up to find some car keys. We'll probably have to abandon our car once we run out of gas."

"Can't we get some at a self-service gas station?"

"Even if it's self-service, I think the attendant has to give permission for you to start pumping gas. We might be able to figure out how it works, but we're now living in a world where we can drive any car we want; we might as well try out a whole bunch."

"Ever the optimist. You really are dead set on making sure you enjoy this world, aren't you…?"

"Things are tough enough without the internet or running water, so we need something to cheer us up," Haruka said with a laugh. Maybe I should follow her example and lean into it a bit more.

"Sure, let's check the zombies' pockets. Still…it'll be hard to travel all over Japan looking for water, so what I really want is to somehow get my hands on a water purifier and set up a base near a river."

"It would help if we came across someone who knows about water purifiers."

"If only life were that easy. Maybe we should get a survival guide from the library to study."

"*Bleh...* Hey, didn't Ichinose say she likes to read?"

"...Maybe we can ask her."

We continued chatting as we carried drinking water to the car, loading it up until we couldn't fit any more. Haruka got in the driver's seat, and we set out for the dorm.

"Yuuma, you can sleep if you like. I'll wake you up if something happens."

"Yeah? Thanks..."

I pushed my seat back a little, closed my heavy eyelids, and fell asleep to the relaxing vibrations of the car...

When I opened my eyes, I was still in the car. The engine was turned off, though, so I guessed we were already back at the dorm.

"Oh, Yuuma. Good morning."

Haruka took her eyes off the map she was studying and smiled.

"How long was I asleep?"

"It's noon now, so about four hours. Everyone helped carry in the water we brought back from the supermarket."

"You should have woken me up..."

"We were making a fair amount of noise, but you didn't even stir. I felt bad for you, so I decided to stay with you until you woke up."

"Oh, thanks. What're you looking at, by the way?"

"It's a map of the prefecture. I thought I'd memorize it in case something happens, since we can't use our phones or GPS."

"You're *memorizing* a map...? Is that even possible...?"

"There's no way I could memorize the whole thing; I'm more remembering locations that can serve as landmarks."

"Ah. That's gonna really come in handy, since I have no sense of direction."

"Hee-hee-hee. Like I said before, you can leave the driving to me."

"That means we'll have to think about protective gear for you. Ichinose suggested wrapping magazines around your arms, but it'd be hard to wear that all the time..."

"We have a million things to do, huh...? Oh, also, Tsukishiro and the others put washtubs and large pots up on the rooftop to collect rainwater. And I found an empty oil drum in the storage room."

"They had an *empty oil drum*?"

"Apparently, they used them as makeshift bathtubs for camping. I also found wooden pallets and bricks, which gave me an idea: We could all go to the river nearby and bathe in the oil drum."

"No way, that sounds too risky. There's no telling when zombies might attack us if we went to an open area like the river."

"I was afraid you'd say that... But should we just give up on bathing because we don't have running water anymore?"

"...What do you mean?"

"You were the one who said we should 'believe tomorrow will be better than today.' If we're going to have hope that we'll survive, we can't keep adding to the number of things we already have to endure."

"...You've got a point."

Maybe we could put up with not having a bath for a few months, but we had to go on living for decades to come. If Tsukishiro and the others never stepped outside the dorm and just spent their days eating the food I brought them, then they could lose their minds sooner or later...

"Let's see if we can find a river that looks safe."

"Thank you, Yuuma! Also, while we're out getting supplies, there's something I want you to do for me. Won't I need a swimsuit if we're going to have a bath by the river?"

"Yeah, true." It wasn't like she could bathe in the open with just a towel to cover her body.

—Not that I'd be against that, but I was sure the girls would object.

"So I want you to clear out a department store for me where I can choose a swimsuit."

"You're kidding, right?"

"All you have to do is tie up all the zombies inside."

"Don't make it sound so easy... I haven't checked out any department stores, but there are probably thousands, maybe even *tens* of thousands of zombies in a place like that."

"Catch ten thousand a day, and you'll be done in a few days."

"You're evil."

"Is that a no...?"

"Of course it's a no. Don't you have a swimsuit at home?"

"We don't have swimming for PE at high school, so I only have the one I used to wear back in junior high. It's the school swimsuit, and it's really tight around my chest..."

"......"

"You just looked at my chest, didn't you?"

"No."

"I'll let it go if you help me find a swimsuit."

"I said I didn't look."

"I want something cute, since I'll be showing it off to you. You'd like to see me in a swimsuit, too, wouldn't you?"

"Not particularly."

"Be honest, or I'll show everyone the video I took and tell them you're my obedient little dog when it's just the two of us."

"…I want to see you in a swimsuit."

"Which would you rather see, me in my school swimsuit or in a bikini?"

"I mean…"

"I also have photos of you in that cage."

"Bikini…!!"

"I thought as much… You do your best to find me a department store, and I'll try to look as cute as possible. I've never worn a bikini before," Haruka said with a shy smile. It seemed like she was convinced I would do anything to see her in a swimsuit.

Not that she was wrong.

"Since it's almost impossible to tie up every zombie in a department store, I'll think of something else," I told her. "Like, what if we found a clothing store where I can get rid of all the zombies…?"

"Yes, please!"

"But that still won't be enough to guarantee your safety, so I'll always make sure I'm by your side whenever you go looking for a swimsuit."

"I'd want nothing less. You can help me pick one out."

In other words, I'd get to accompany Haruka when she went looking for a swimsuit…!!

That was all the motivation I needed.

"—Wouldn't you all like to take a bath?"

It was just after three in the afternoon, and Haruka had gathered everyone in the cafeteria to tell them our idea.

"...What do you mean, Hyuuga? Didn't we agree not to use the bath since we can't use the tap water anymore?"

"I'm glad you asked, Tsukishiro. Thanks to all of Yuuma's hard work, we can now use a drum bath. And that's not all; there's also a clothing store where we can pick up bathing suits."

Haruka explained to the other three girls that I'd gone to the river nearby and tied up all the zombies lurking about, found a small pickup truck to take the oil drum to the riverbed where I'd set it up, and found and secured a clothing store.

"So anyone who wants to take a bath can come with us down to the river. Tell us if you want to go out."

"......"

Our three dorm mates looked at each other with confusion. I couldn't blame them; how could anyone say yes to a suggestion like that on the spot?

"...You're asking if we're willing to risk our lives to take a bath...," Tsukishiro mumbled.

When she put it that way, I saw that we were asking them to make a huge decision...

"Okay. Then Yuuma and I will go today, and once we know it's safe, you can all go tomorrow—"

"Absolutely not," Tsukishiro said flatly. "We're all working together to survive. We can't keep letting the two of you risk your lives for our sakes..."

"It's not that big of a deal," I said. "It was just an idea Haruka came up with because she was thinking about herself."

"Um... I wouldn't mind going," Lisa chimed in. "It's tough being unable to take a bath for such a long time, but there's more to it than that... I think it's about time I got a look at what's going on with the outside world."

"…If it isn't too much trouble, I'd also like to come," Ichinose said with a determined look. "We can't stay in here until we die, and this sounds like a good opportunity…"

"Then it's decided: All five of us will go out today," Tsukishiro said, every bit of hesitation gone from her expression. Lisa and Ichinose nodded.

Our three dorm mates had readied themselves to venture into the outside world.

We grabbed a change of clothes, then got in the car and headed to the clothing store with Haruka driving. But as soon as we left the dormitory—

"…It really is a mess…," Lisa said, overwhelmed as she took in the bizarre sight. She was sitting on the right side of the back seat. "It looks like something out of a video game… I hadn't quite believed it up till now, but it's real…"

Lisa hadn't been outside once since the zombies first appeared. She sat there looking out the car window, and it seemed like the reality of the situation had finally sunk in.

The same went for Ichinose, sitting on the left side in the back. She silently stared at the zombies roaming the road and the charred husks of crashed cars.

Tsukishiro sat in the middle between Lisa and Ichinose, and she didn't even attempt to look outside. She'd been guarding the gate all this time, but she was probably running on fumes…

We eventually arrived at the clothing store where I'd cleaned out the zombies. I first went in alone, to check that it was safe, then invited the others to join me.

We were walking toward the swimsuit section when Haruka came up to me and asked teasingly, "What sort of swimsuits do you like?"

"Why do you want to know?"

"I'll use that to help me pick."

"Just choose whatever you like."

"Hey, I'm going out of my way to ask what you like because I'm such a nice person."

"What do you want me to say…?"

I wondered how to react to that as I gazed at the swimsuits on display.

To be honest, I thought Haruka would look cute in any of them, but if I had to choose, I'd prefer one that revealed as much as possible. After all, it wasn't like I had to worry about other guys seeing her.

Still, I didn't have the courage to say that to Haruka. I didn't want to lie and say I liked more covered-up swimsuits, either, though. It was a tough question to answer…

"Are you having trouble picking one when there's so many to choose from?" Haruka commented pointedly with a half smile.

"I never said that," I denied automatically. "And why do you need to limit yourself to one in the first place anyway? Wouldn't it make more sense to get a few if you're going to wear one to take a bath every day?"

If she had to wear them anyway, I thought it might be nice to see her in a variety of swimwear, but Haruka just pouted at me.

"Don't be such a downer when I'm having fun choosing a swimsuit."

"You're the one who dragged me into this."

"Fine then, I'll choose one myself. At least tell me what colors you like."

"Hmm…"

I took another look at the swimsuits on the racks. Haruka would probably try to find a swimsuit in whatever colors I told her I liked. That said, I didn't have the faintest idea of which to choose. Black and white seemed nice, but red and blue also suited her…

"If I had to choose, pink and light blue."

For some reason, Haruka seemed at a loss for words. Then after an odd pause, she hesitantly asked, "You're thinking of the underwear I was wearing, aren't you?"

"—Huh?!"

"I wore light blue yesterday and pink the day before that."

It was only after that statement that I remembered her pink bra and light blue panties.

"N-no, I'm not! That's just a coincidence!"

Haruka looked at me suspiciously. "There's no way that could be a coincidence."

She was absolutely right. I had no room to argue.

"Don't tell me that seeing my underwear changed your preferences?"

"……"

"What?! Am I right?!"

"What can I say…? No comment."

"I—I see… So your list of favorite colors is going to grow every time I let you see my underwear, is it?" Haruka murmured. Her cheeks were flushed, and a complicated expression creased her face.

*She must think I'm a pervert…*

"…Okay, I've heard your request. I'll try on the pink and light-blue swimsuits, so wait here," she said shyly.

Haruka began picking out the bathing suits she'd try on in the fitting room, so I moved away from the swimsuit section, figuring it wouldn't be a good idea to stare too closely.

As I wandered around the rest of the store, I passed Lisa, who was filling up her shopping basket. It wasn't just swimsuits; she seemed to be getting a lot of regular clothes, too.

She smiled shyly when she saw me looking. "It's free, right? So I thought I'd take a bunch of different stuff while I'm here."

"Good idea. It's better to have a lot of clothes, since it'll be hard to do laundry."

"Right? I really owe you one. My breasts keep getting bigger lately, so my bras have gotten tight."

"Y-you don't say..."

Not sure how to react, my eyes automatically went to her chest.

All of a sudden, a shock ran down my spine. I turned around to see Haruka standing there staring at me and realized she'd head-butted me from behind.

"This one's nice. What do you think? It's pink, your favorite."

Haruka was holding the swimsuit over her clothes, but it was a fairly revealing pink bikini. What was there not to like?

"I don't know much about women's clothing, but I reckon it'd look good on you."

"Okay, I'll try it on, and you can tell me what you think. Wait for me outside the fitting rooms. And don't wander around." For some reason, that last bit sounded like a warning.

"Don't you think it'd be strange for me to wait outside the fitting rooms?"

"...Yeah, you've got a point. In that case, maintain an appropriate distance from the fitting rooms and wait for me there with your eyes and ears closed until I come back."

With that fearsome order, Haruka stepped into the fitting room and closed the curtain.

...Trying on a swimsuit meant she'd take off all her clothes. Didn't she feel uneasy with only a single flimsy curtain between us? I could probably sneak a peek if there was a gap somewhere... However, Haruka had made sure to close the curtain all the way, so an accident seemed unlikely. There went that idea.

As I was making my observations, I saw Lisa add a pink swimsuit to her basket and enter one of the fitting rooms. Meanwhile, Tsukishiro and Ichinose didn't seem to be making much progress in the way of choosing swimsuits, and I listened in on their conversation.

Tsukishiro stood there gazing at a huge selection of swimwear. "This is my first time choosing a swimsuit without being told what to buy by my school. What criteria should I take into account selecting one...?"

"...I've only ever had school swimsuits as well, but considering we'll be washing our bodies wearing them, it might be best to choose something that reveals more skin and has fewer decorations..."

"I see. Thank you for your valuable advice," Tsukishiro said, sounding convinced. She reached for a bikini. "I must admit I'm somewhat hesitant to wear this, but it's a small sacrifice to make given the circumstances. I'll have to wash it once I'm back at the dorm, and the most important thing is for it to be practical..."

"Y-yeah, you're right...," Ichinose replied in a thin, reedy voice, before picking out one for herself. "I'll try on a bikini, too, since you are..."

"Then, shall we make our way to the fitting rooms?"

"Uh-huh..."

It looked like they'd both reached a decision. It was an amazing situation I'd found myself in, witnessing girls pick out their first bikinis...

"Gueeess who!"

Lost in thought, I was suddenly blindfolded from behind.

"Haruka, you're the only one who would do something like this to me."

I lifted her hands off my face, turned around, and saw an angel standing there. The pink material covered the bare minimum of skin; I could stare as much as I wanted at her cleavage, belly button, thighs—and almost everything else.

I knew she'd call me out for harassment if I stared at her for too long, but I just couldn't take my eyes off Haruka's body.

*Damn... She looks so cute...!! I wish she never takes this off...!!*

"...Yuuma, you're staring," Haruka complained, covering her breasts with her hands. "Geez...you have such a dirty mind..."

Seeing Haruka pouting at me, I regained my senses and quickly looked away.

"...Sorry. I don't know what came over me."

"Oh, well, it's okay. It just means I look so amazing in this swimsuit that you lost your mind."

"N-no, it's not like that..."

"Do you honestly believe you can bluff your way out of this after staring at me like that? Your eyes kept going up and down, back and forth, over and over again."

"......"

"Hee-hee! You're so cute, Yuuma."

Haruka smiled victoriously and removed her hands from her chest. I didn't know whether that meant she didn't mind if I kept looking, but I wasn't going to do that again.

Just then, the curtain to another fitting room opened, and Lisa came out wearing a swimsuit. She had on a pink bikini, and her body was almost more than I could handle.

Lisa's eyes met mine, and she dashed over to me, those huge boobs bigger than Haruka's bouncing up and down. "What do you think of this swimsuit, Yuuma?"

"Huh…? Uh… I think it's nice…," I mumbled incoherently, and Lisa took a step toward me. She stood on tiptoe and whispered in my ear, so close I could feel her breath brush against me, "Who looks cuter, me or Hyuuga?"

My gaze automatically went to them, comparing Haruka and Lisa. I knew I shouldn't, but I just couldn't look away—

Then Tsukishiro walked out of another fitting room. She'd also changed into a bikini, of course, and I found my eyes irresistibly drawn to her.

"—!!"

But as soon as Tsukishiro's eyes met mine, she quickly went back inside the fitting room and closed the curtain. What in the world was going on…?

I suddenly felt a tug on my right arm. It was Haruka, as usual.

"Yuuma, have you chosen a bathing suit for yourself?"

"Not yet—"

"We can't have that. Let's pick one out right now!"

She grabbed my arm and pulled me away. It pained me to leave, and I tried to turn back around, but when I did, Haruka bent my pointer finger at an awkward angle.

"Yuuma. Watch where you're going. It's dangerous."

"Isn't it more dangerous to have someone try to break your finger while you walk…?"

"Hmm? Did you say something?"

"No, nothing at all…"

I could hear the anger clearly in Haruka's voice, so I let her drag me away without any further provocation.

The men's swimwear section was relatively small, with far less variety than the women's section.

"Okay, I'll pick out some swimwear for you."

"I'm good with anything."

"Then let's get that one; that's pretty much just a string that barely covers your private parts."

"Be serious, okay? Don't go too crazy."

In the end, I chose a pair of simple, navy blue swim trunks, like the kind I'd worn for swimming class at school. I grabbed a few spares and carried my five identical pairs of shorts back to the fitting rooms, where the others had already finished changing back into their uniforms.

"Too bad, Yuuma," Haruka said, suppressing a laugh, but I pretended not to have any idea what she was talking about.

After Haruka also got changed, the five of us hopped in the car and left.

The first thing I did when we arrived at the riverbank was to go out by myself and take a look around, but I couldn't see any zombies anywhere. Since the zombie outbreak had started on a weekday afternoon, there probably hadn't been many people out here in the first place, which meant relatively few zombies.

I returned to the car and led the others down the embankment.

"—Wow! Kousaka, did you set everything up by yourself?" Tsukishiro asked, wide-eyed.

To save us some time, I'd laid out the bricks for the foundation of the bath and placed the drum on top when I'd come earlier.

"I'm amazed that you managed to do this all by yourself..."

"It's no big deal."

That was a lie. The huge oil drum probably weighed more than twenty kilos, so it would've been a pain to move if I hadn't turned myself into a zombie.

But when Haruka looked at me, I could see envy in her eyes.

"...Yuuma. Please don't try to use every opportunity you get to make yourself popular with women."

"I told you: I'm not."

"Now, then," Tsukishiro continued, "let's get to work. Ichinose and I will be responsible for starting the fire. Hyuuga and Hoshimiya, can you two fetch water from the river and fill the drum until it's about seventy percent full? It can hold up to two hundred liters, so we'll need one hundred and forty liters of water. Kousaka, please keep an eye out in case any zombies show up."

"Got it."

With our roles divvied up, we got to work. My job was just to stand watch, though, so I observed what everyone else was doing. Tsukishiro and Ichinose tried to light the firewood using a pack of fire starters they'd brought from the shed, but it didn't appear to be working. Haruka and Lisa carried buckets back and forth between the river and drum bath, filling it up. They could carry about two liters of water at a time, which meant they'd have to make thirty-five trips each...

Eventually, the fire caught and began to heat the bottom of the drum, but it didn't seem very strong. Having finished fetching the water, Haruka checked the thermometer in the bath with a despondent look.

"It isn't warming up at all... I wonder how long it'll take before we can go in."

Ichinose pulled out a pen and notebook and started doing some calculations. There were a lot of symbols there I'd never seen before, so I had no idea what she was writing.

"Based on the current water temperature, it will probably take around three hours."

"*Three hours...?!*"

The sun would go down if we waited that long, and considering the possibility of zombies showing up, we wanted to pack up and leave before it got dark.

We had to do something.

"I have an idea," Haruka said. "How about we reduce the amount of water in the drum? I think we can make do with less water if we bathe in pairs."

But Tsukishiro spoke up against her idea.

"That means Kousaka will have to bathe alone, and there won't be enough water."

"That's okay!" replied Haruka. "I'll go in with him!"

We agreed to go with Haruka's idea for today, though it still took more than an hour for the water to reach thirty-eight degrees Celsius. Starting tomorrow, we'd have to use a portable gas burner or find some other way to shorten the time it took to heat the bath.

"The water's just about ready," Tsukishiro announced. "Why don't we go and change into our bathing suits?"

"We're going to take turns getting changed in the car, right?" I asked.

"You can see in through the windows, but I'll make sure Yuuma doesn't look, so don't worry about changing," Haruka told the group. I really wished she wouldn't say something like that; it would only make everyone feel insecure.

Tsukishiro gave me a gentle smile. "It's okay. Everyone here trusts you. Now then, who wants to get changed first?"

"Oh, uh, I'm already wearing my swimming trunks underneath my clothes." I hadn't taken them off when I'd tried them on at the store.

"What a coincidence. I'm still wearing my swimsuit, too," Lisa said, pulling her T-shirt up to her belly button.

I knew she was wearing a bikini underneath, but I still couldn't help swallowing.

"Then Hyuuga, Ichinose, and I will need to get changed in the car."

"As the owner of the car, I'll go first," Haruka said. "It should be okay, since we're this far away from the car, but please check to make sure you can't see me inside."

She went running to the car she'd parked at the top of the embankment, and naturally, I immediately looked away.

*...Any second now, Haruka's going to be completely naked inside that car...*

But no sooner had that thought flashed through my mind than Lisa pulled off her T-shirt to reveal the pink bikini top I'd seen back at that store. I followed suit, doing my best not to look in her direction. Haruka still wasn't back yet, but Lisa and I were already fully changed into our bathing suits.

"...Hey, Yuuma. Would you mind getting in the drum bath for a sec so I can see how high the water rises with one person?" Lisa asked out of nowhere.

True, we could probably bathe in less water, in which case I wouldn't have to sit in the drum with Haruka in front of everyone. I made up my mind to get in the warm water and try it out for real.

I took off my shoes, climbed the short three-step aluminum ladder, and slipped a foot into the hot water. I'd set the wooden pallet underneath the bottom of the drum, so I didn't think I'd burn myself.

There wasn't as much water in there as I'd thought there would be. I put both my feet in the drum bath and stood up, but the water only came to around my waist.

"Figures. I thought it might be tough for one person to bathe in there," Lisa said. She'd taken off her shoes and was now standing on the stepladder looking inside the drum.

"I wonder, if two people go in, will the water come up to our shoulders? Okay, scooch a bit."

"—Huh?!"

Lisa lowered herself into the drum without waiting for me to reply. She was in her bikini, and we were so close to each other that I was almost touching her…

"Hmm. Even with both of us, the water only comes up to our stomachs. It should come up higher if we squat down."

As soon as the words left her lips, she kneeled in the drum, her knees sliding between my open legs. And any time she moved, two ample mounds rubbed my thighs.

"Hey!! What do you think you're doing?!"

A high-pitched yell reached us from the top of the embankment; Haruka had finished changing and gotten out of the car to see me and Lisa in the bath together. She came running toward us with incredible intensity.

"Yuuma, you're taking a bath with me, aren't you?!"

"Oh, sorry," Lisa apologized. "I wanted to test it out first. I can pair up with Yuuma instead, if you want."

"It's okay! I'll swap with you right now if you'll kindly get out!"

"Sure. Oh, but would you mind waiting until I warm up a bit?"

"Fine! You don't have to get out right away, but please move away from Yuuma!"

"There's not much water in here, though. I can't soak up to my shoulders unless I kneel."

"Then I'll join you, so the water rises!"

Haruka kicked off her shoes, got up on the stepladder, and forced her way into the small space behind me. Lisa stood up to make sure she had enough room for herself, but it was still way too cramped for the three of us to bathe together.

Lisa's breasts were pushed up against my body from the front, while Haruka's pressed into my back...!!

I couldn't believe what was happening. The water temperature wasn't supposed to be above forty degrees Celsius, but my body felt like it was on fire.

"Aren't you warmer now, Hoshimiya?"

"Mm, maybe if I wait a bit longer."

"Shouldn't you step out and sit by the fire if you're that cold?"

"Well, now that we have this bath, I'd like to warm up in the hot water."

The two girls continued arguing back and forth, with me in the middle. Every time they moved I could feel a sublime softness through the thin material of their swimsuits.

*What's going on? Is this heaven? Did I die? Well, I guess I pretty much did, since I turned into a zombie...*

"A drum bath is no place to play around!" Tsukishiro yelled, seeing the two girls bicker. "What if you burn yourselves while you're messing around?! There are no longer any hospitals or clinics in this world!"

"S-sorry…" She was so angry I ended up apologizing along with Lisa and Haruka.

"Hyuuga, Hoshimiya, the two of you are causing problems, so *neither* of you are allowed to bathe with Kousaka. Come out of there right this minute."

"But then the water won't come up to Yuuma's shoulders…"

"You don't need to worry about that; I'll bathe with Kousaka."

*—What?!*

Tsukishiro seemed serious about it, though, because she kicked the other two out of the bath and quickly went to the car to get changed.

When she came back, she wasn't wearing the bathing suit she'd tried on at the store, but a sophisticated white bikini. It didn't show off as much skin as Haruka's and Lisa's swimsuits and, combined with her hesitant expression, gave off a pure, clean-cut vibe.

Tsukishiro sank into the water and turned to face me.

"…This is embarrassing," she said awkwardly and covered her chest with her hands. I didn't know where to look…

"I'm sorry you had to do this…"

"Kousaka, please don't apologize. It's not your fault. And besides…I don't particularly mind…"

"Th-that's good."

Tsukishiro smiled shyly. "…It seems like Hyuuga and Hoshimiya are competing over you. You can pair up with me the next time we do something like this."

*Does that mean I'll be taking a bath with her every day…?*

"…Uh, my body's plenty warm now, so the next person can take a bath."

By the time I got out, I hadn't even been in the bath with Tsukishiro for three minutes. The awkwardness of standing there face-to-face in our swimsuits was just too much—as were the heated gazes we attracted from the others.

Ichinose also changed into her bathing suit after that, and the girls took turns soaking in the drum bath. I was watching them offhandedly when Haruka, who'd already finished bathing, pulled my ear and dragged me a short distance away.

"Yuuma, you're staring." It was a warning... "Also, I think you're getting too close to Hoshimiya. The next time she asks you to take a bath with her, you have to refuse her more firmly."

"But we're dorm mates who live under the same roof."

"That only gets you so far. As your girlfriend, I worry when you do something like go in the drum bath with her."

"—Huh?!"

Haruka's words were so unexpected my brain stopped working for a few seconds.

She raised her eyebrows. "Did I say something funny?"

"Uh, no, it's just..."

She *had* said she'd be my girlfriend when we thought I'd turn into a zombie and die, but...

"What you said about going out with me... That's still happening?"

Haruka's eyes widened, and she let out a noise close to a scream.

"—What?! Of course it is!!"

"Sorry. I thought it was all just a joke."

"...Seeing as you're a zombie, you don't mind if I strangle you for about ten hours, right?"

"I do mind, actually."

I wish she'd stop saying scary things like that so matter-of-factly.

"I—I mean, that was when we thought I was about to die, right? So I guess I just assumed it was null and void when I managed to survive..."

"If it was, then I wouldn't be sleeping in the same room as you, and I wouldn't have laughed it off and forgiven you when you looked up my skirt."

"I guess I just thought you were cool with stuff like that."

"Since you're a zombie, you don't mind if I shave off all your hair, do you?"

"Please stop suggesting things that have nothing to do with zombies."

"If you don't want to be bald, you can make it up to me by telling everyone we're going out."

"Why do I have to do that?"

"To make sure no one else gets any funny ideas about seducing you. Now, let's go see the others and tell them you're head over heels for me."

"Don't you think that'd be weird, suddenly announcing something like that? And what do you mean *seducing me*?"

"Like when you and Hoshimiya were all alone in the bath, obviously."

"She just wanted to see what it would be like for two people to go in at the same time."

"Does becoming a zombie suddenly make you dumb?"

"That's simple but mean."

…But I suppose it was natural for a girl to worry about her boyfriend. I'd probably be just as frustrated if I were in her shoes…

"I'm sorry. I'll refuse next time if you don't like it… But I don't want to tell the others about us, since they'll only start worrying."

"…Hee-hee-hee. That sounds like something a guy would say to his girlfriend." Haruka smiled. "Okay, I'll forgive you this time since you finally seem to have figured out how to act as my boyfriend. However…if something like this happens again, *I'll break it.*"

"Break…*what?*"

Once everyone had finally finished bathing, we put out the fire that was heating the bath, threw out the water, and headed home. We left the drum where it was since we'd be using it again tomorrow and every day after that.

It might be because it was everyone's first time outside in a while and we'd enjoyed an outdoor bath, which was out of the ordinary, but the mood in the car was upbeat on the way home. Haruka was right; it was a good thing we hadn't given up on taking baths. Times were tough, which was exactly why we had to try to enjoy every little morsel of happiness we could find.

But once we returned to the dorm, we found that the lights wouldn't go on.

I quickly went to the dining room and checked the main breaker, but I couldn't see anything wrong with it.

"…Kousaka. Look," Ichinose said, pointing out the window. "It's starting to go dark outside, but the streetlights aren't coming on."

"You're right… I didn't notice that at all…"

The blackout seemed to be affecting the whole area. Were the power lines damaged somewhere? Or had the power plant that'd been going strong up till now finally stopped working?

We used our phones to illuminate the cafeteria, eating dinner in the dim light. However, from now on, we wouldn't be able to use the induction cooktops, the microwave, or the refrigerator, so all the frozen food we'd brought back from the supermarket would thaw out.

"For dinner tonight, let's just have canned foods and other things we don't need to prepare," Tsukishiro said, quickly coming to grips with the situation and focusing on the possibilities available to us. "Kousaka, it would be a great help if you could find a portable stove somewhere tomorrow."

"Okay. I'll also get us a bunch of flashlights."

"Could you pick up some scented candles, while you're at it?" Haruka added, relaxed as usual. "Are you going to go out to get it now?"

"No, it's too dark outside, and I don't want to risk an accident, so I'll wait and go tomorrow. It might be good if we could all try to think about what we need now that the power's out."

Having laid out the plan, we started to eat, which was more difficult to do in the dark room than I'd imagined. For one, getting the food to your mouth accurately is a hassle. On top of that, you can't really taste food when you can't see it, so it's easy to sink into a depression.

I was getting a headache just thinking about how our lives would be starting tomorrow...

"This is kind of fun," Haruka said brightly. "It's like we're camping. Tomorrow, let's bring tents and sleeping bags. Oh, and a telescope, since we should be able to see the stars clearly with the city pitch-black."

Our one saving grace was Haruka's unwavering optimism. Although, maybe she had a little *too much* energy…

After some struggle, we managed to finish our meal, and we all returned to our rooms. It was too dark to do anything, so we ended up going to bed early.

Tomorrow, as soon as the sun was up, I'd go out looking for supplies…

…A little while after falling asleep, I dreamed of a woman letting out a long, piercing cry. It was followed by Tsukishiro's screaming voice, which seemed to come from a long way away. She sounded distraught, and it was hard to imagine the calm, collected girl I knew making a sound like that. Next, I heard the panicked footsteps of two people getting closer. They were coming from the entrance to the dorm and heading straight for my room—

The door slammed open.

All the disturbing sounds I'd been hearing were real.

Sensing the unusual atmosphere around me, I instinctively sat up in bed. Tsukishiro stood in the doorway, the light from her phone turned toward me, and I noticed a woman standing next to her. She was wearing a suit and looked to be in her early twenties.

"—Yuuma!! The gate!!"

I was still drowsy and couldn't think straight. But Tsukishiro sounded so frantic that something terrible must have happened.

I grabbed the hemp rope I kept by my pillow and staggered out of bed.

"This lady came to the dorm!! There were so many zombies when I opened the gate!! I couldn't close it!!"

"—I understand."

Now that I had the basic gist of the problem, I slipped past Tsukishiro and the other woman and ran out of the room in bare feet. The hallway was dark, and I could barely see a thing, but I heard indistinct moans coming from somewhere not too far away.

There were zombies nearby. Several of them.

I ran back to my room, woke up Haruka, and put on a spare pair of shoes.

*Why did this have to happen right after the power went out, of all times...?*

"I'm so sorry... This is all my fault...," Tsukishiro apologized tearfully and collapsed on the spot. She must've thought this would be the end for us.

I gently patted her on the head. "It's going to be okay. I'll take care of everything."

She gazed up at me with a look of surprise, and I smiled.

"You were just trying to help someone. No one can blame you for that."

With that, I reached for my metal baseball bat.

*—Now, then.*

I was acting cool, but there were a million things to do. I needed to protect Haruka and the two others in my room, meet up with Lisa and Ichinose upstairs, while also going out to close the gate. What was the best way to do all—?

*Crash!!*

Suddenly, the window facing the yard shattered. I shone the light from my phone toward it and saw a middle-aged, male zombie trying to get inside. I immediately launched myself at him, forced him outside, tied up his arms and legs, and put him on the ground. My room was no longer safe. That said, it was too dangerous to go out into the dark hallway with no idea of how many zombies were out there.

I brushed off the shards of glass and opened the window, coming to the conclusion that it was safer for us to go outside in the moonlight.

I put shoes on Haruka, who was still half asleep, and led her and the other two out into the yard. Unfortunately, though, we'd timed it badly, as just then clouds covered the moon, making it impossible to see where the zombies were. Protecting the three of them while trying to make it to the front gate would be next to impossible.

I would've been able to be a little reckless if I was alone, but I wasn't sure they'd be safe if I left the girls inside. Even if Haruka and Tsukishiro *were* both carrying metal bats they'd found in a room...

Just then, Haruka put down her bat and started running as if she'd thought of something.

I immediately realized what she wanted to do. She jumped in the car without any regard for the risks involved and started the engine.

The darkness cleared, and we saw the zombies.

They reacted to the light and to the sound of the engine and made their way toward the car. I had to tie them up quickly, or they'd surround it—

But just as I was about to run toward them, the driver's side window opened and Haruka shouted out to me.

"Yuuma! You don't have to come over here!"

"Huh?! What do you—?"

"I know you can't kill zombies!! So I will!!"

Haruka suddenly stepped on the gas and sent all the zombies

around her flying. The car seemed to come to a stop, then Haruka started backing up, mowing down the zombies that were coming at her from behind.

Some of them appeared to be okay, but others had had their heads crushed by the tires. Haruka kept going forward and backward, targeting the zombies around her and trying to incapacitate as many as she could.

This was a war between humans and zombies. In which case, Haruka's actions must have been the right thing to do.

—I couldn't afford to hesitate. If I didn't act now, someone would die.

I picked up the bat that Haruka had dropped and took a full swing at the head of the nearest zombie. It was a gross feeling, like bone shattering and something soft being squashed, but it would take more than one swing to destroy its brain.

"Aaaaahh!!"

Yelling at the top of my lungs, I rained down blows on the zombie in front of me. Something that stunk of decay—blood or intestines, I wasn't sure what—splattered every time I swung the bat. The zombie's head must've been crushed by then, but it was too dark to see whether I'd finished the job.

Meanwhile, other zombies were getting closer.

—*It's dark, so I doubt they'll see me.*

I gritted my teeth, turned my back to Tsukishiro and the others, and morphed myself into a zombie.

When I swung the metal bat again, I blew away the zombie's head with a single blow. My strength as a zombie really was incredible. I destroyed one zombie after the next, hidden by the darkness.

I had to protect my friends. I wasn't going to hesitate anymore.

The area was soon covered by the bodies of headless zombies, so I figured it should be safe enough to move away from Tsukishiro and the woman for a little while. Haruka was still fighting fiercely in the car, and with the light of her headlights to see by, I made it to the gate and locked it.

A considerable number of zombies had already entered the dormitory grounds, though. I had to get back to Tsukishiro and the woman as quickly as possible, and also meet up with Lisa and Ichinose—

That was when I saw it.

Until then, it had been too dark to notice the gigantic male zombie standing in my way looking down at me. He was well over three meters tall—basically a huge wall—and the hair on my body stood on end as I looked up at him. My instincts were warning me that this guy was dangerous.

"Tsukishiro! Go back into the room through the window from earlier!"

She should be safe once she went inside and locked the door, since I'd taken care of all the zombies around us. The important thing was to get my friends away from this monster—

"Raaaargh!!"

The giant zombie roared and came charging at me.

I set my sights on its approaching fist and reflexively swung the bat. I thought I'd start off by crushing his right hand—but the monster's arm was as hard as a rock, and the bat bounced right off.

*Calm down. It's moving, so it shouldn't be hard all over.*

I decided to aim for a different body part. Without hesitating for a moment, I got inside the zombie's guard and swung the bat at his left knee. The contact was met with a feeling like a ceramic plate shattering, and the giant zombie lost his balance.

*I can't let up here—*

But just as that thought flashed through my mind, something

passed in front of my eyes. A moment too late, I realized it was the zombie's right arm.

The monster's fist made contact, tearing off my right hand from the wrist down, and my hand went flying, still holding the bat. A shiver went down my spine. If the zombie hadn't lost his balance just then, it would've been my head that went flying.

If I had the choice, I'd run right here and now—but I had people to protect. I had to do something about this monster.

Still, losing my right hand was a huge blow. How could I fight this monster with only my left hand?

"Yuuma!! Get out of the way!!"

My vision suddenly went completely white. A moment later, I realized it was the headlights from the car.

Haruka had rammed into the giant zombie from behind.

I jumped to the side not a moment too soon, and Haruka ran over the zombie at full speed. His huge body was lifted up by the hood of the car, and the back of his head hit the windshield with an almighty crash, leaving a spiderweb-like crack in the glass.

I couldn't waste the opening Haruka had risked her life to create for me. I picked up the baseball bat with my left hand and jumped onto the chest of the zombie as lay face up on the hood.

*First, I'll crush his eyeballs—*

But the giant zombie grabbed the raised bat. Try as I might, it wouldn't budge; even with my zombie strength, I was no match for this monster.

I thrust my right arm—sans hand—in front of his face, trying to use the blood spurting from the wound to obscure the zombie's vision. But with blinding speed, the monster raised his upper body and tore off my right arm with his teeth. Before I knew what'd happened, he had bitten off my arm all the way to my elbow and swallowed it.

His clouded eyes turned toward me. I could almost feel him mocking me.

It was over. There was no way I could defeat something like this—

However, the gigantic zombie suddenly let out an agonized groan. He let go of the bat, shook me off, leaned forward, and spat out my arm.

I had no idea what was happening, but this was my one-in-a-million chance to take this thing down. I aimed for his head and swung the bat as hard as I could.

"—Haruka!!"

"On it!!"

It seemed Haruka had understood me perfectly, because she backed up the car, then slammed her foot on the gas. She knocked the giant's body down to the ground, then crushed his head with the left front wheel.

We couldn't let a monster like that come back to life. Once Haruka moved the car, and I made sure the giant zombie was dead, I completely destroyed his head so he would never move again.

Although our greatest threat was gone, we couldn't relax just yet. We still had to wipe out all the zombies that'd entered the dorm grounds.

First, I picked up my torn-off right hand and arm. When I put the open wounds against one another, not only did they attach in a matter of seconds, but I could also move them around without any problems. I'd had no idea that my body would be able to regenerate so well. Zombies' bodies really are amazing…!!

But this wasn't the time to focus on something like that. Now that I could hold my bat in both hands again, I went back inside and began taking care of the remaining zombies. Halfway through the process, I realized I was no longer feeling any resistance to killing them, but I decided to put it out of my mind for now.

It only took about another ten minutes to finish exterminating all the zombies on the first floor, and I went back out into the yard. Haruka had her head out the driver's side window and was pointing up into the sky. I looked up where she was indicating and was relieved to see Lisa and Ichinose peeking out of the window. They were safe.

"There might still be more zombies in the dorm! Lock the door, and don't open it until I get there!" I shouted up to them, and the girls replied with a thumbs-up.

From this point on, I had to make sure I did things in the right order. First, I would take Tsukishiro and the woman somewhere safe, then check to see if there were still any zombies inside the dorm, and finally I'd meet up with Lisa and Ichinose.

"Haruka, you stay here. Watch the gate and keep the engine running. I'll bring Tsukishiro and the woman who showed up asking for help to the car."

"Okay."

"Honk if anything happens, and I'll come running."

I returned to the dorm and opened the door to the room where Tsukishiro and the woman were hiding.

"The ground floor is safe, at least for now. I'm going to check the other floors, so I want you both to wait with Haruka in the car," I said into the dark room. The two of them nodded, and the mystery woman stepped out into the hallway, followed by Tsukishiro.

I took the lead and headed for the yard where Haruka was waiting, all the while watching for zombies hiding in the shadows.

* * *

"—Watch out!!"

Tsukishiro suddenly yelled out from behind me, and I was pushed forward.

I turned around, confused, and saw the mystery woman biting Tsukishiro's upper arm.

Her skin had turned gray. It had been too dark to notice earlier, but she'd turned into a zombie. She must've been bitten before coming here. I should've anticipated something like this happening!

Cursing my carelessness, I pulled the zombie away from Tsukishiro and wrestled her to the floor.

"Damn you!! How could you do that?!"

I caved her head in with the baseball bat and immediately turned to Tsukishiro. She was slumped to the floor, clearly having trouble breathing.

"Sorry about this, but I'm going to take your top off."

I removed the upper part of her archery uniform and saw a painful-looking bite mark high up on her right arm. The wound was deep, so there was no doubt she'd been infected...

I had no idea what to say to her...

But as I fell silent, Tsukishiro smiled.

"I'm glad...that you're okay..."

"Tsukishiro—"

"It's more important for everyone's sakes that you survive instead of me... So don't feel bad..." Tsukishiro's voice was weak, and her face contorted in pain.

...I'd never even imagined that something like this might happen.

If only I'd explained to her that I'd been fine after being bitten by a zombie...

I took Tsukishiro in my arms and went back inside the room we'd just left. I laid her down on the bed, but she was barely breathing anymore, and I used my phone to give us some light.

"Can you see me?"

"...Yes..."

"I want you to calmly listen to what I'm about to tell you. I can turn myself into a zombie."

I'd dropped a bombshell, but Tsukishiro didn't even react.

"I don't blame you if you don't believe me. But—" I went ahead and turned myself into a zombie and could see Tsukishiro swallow. "It's true. That's why I'm fine, even if I get bitten... I'm really sorry I hid this from you..."

"I...see..."

"I know an apology at this point isn't going to make you less angry, and I'll take any punishment you throw at me, so just please, live through this. There's a chance that, like me, you won't lose your consciousness. You have to stay strong."

I held her hand and tried to cheer her up, but Tsukishiro's body temperature was rapidly dropping. This was exactly how it had happened to me...

"...Kousaka. Please don't worry about me dying."

"But..."

As I hesitated, Tsukishiro looked at me with a strong gaze.

"—I've been in love with you ever since you first came to us."

"...Huh...?!"

"Even in a difficult situation like this, you think of others…and protect them… You are a man worthy of respect…"

"You're wrong. That's not who I really am. The real me is a coward who deceives people and—"

"Even if you've been hiding the fact that you're a zombie, you've still been doing everything you can to help me… You never abused your power… That is noble of you…"

"…But because I lied to you, you…"

"…I didn't think I would ever confess my feelings for you, because you have Hyuuga… But now that I'm about to die, I can tell you how I truly feel, which makes me happy."

"…Tsukishiro…"

"May I ask you to do me one last favor…?"

"Of course. Anything you want."

"…I don't want you to see me as a zombie, so please, kill me now."

"…I can't do that…"

But Tsukishiro's skin was becoming grayer by the minute. She didn't have much time left.

There had to be some way to save her… How could I be the only person to turn into a zombie and still maintain my consciousness?

Just then, a memory of my fight with the giant zombie earlier flashed through my mind—when it had swallowed my arm and immediately started writhing in agony.

Unlike other zombies, I hadn't lost my self-awareness. Could that be because there was some kind of special bacteria in my body fighting the virus? Was that why the giant zombie had looked to be in pain after drinking my blood?

If I was right, then I could give Tsukishiro that bacteria—

"Tsukishiro, there's something I want to try! Tsukishiro!"

But she just stared at me vacantly without responding. Her

skin had turned completely gray, and her eyes were starting to cloud over.

Would she be able to drink my blood in her current state? Was there some other way I could give her the bacteria in my body?

—*I could get her to drink my saliva.*

When a zombie bit a person, they were infected by the virus contained in its saliva, so there was a good chance the same went for the anti-zombie virus in my body.

There was no time to lose. I instinctively pressed my mouth against Tsukishiro's, pried open the gap between her top and bottom teeth with my tongue, and desperately forced my saliva into her mouth.

"Tsukishiro! Swallow, please!"

"...Ngh...!"

Despite her pain, Tsukishiro managed to swallow some. I didn't know how much she'd need to overcome the virus, though, so I kept feeding her more and more of my saliva...

......I had no idea how much time went by.

A while after I began feeding her my saliva, Tsukishiro's cloudy eyes slowly returned to their original color, and her body temperature gradually started to rise. Her condition seemed to have improved, so I stopped kissing her.

As soon as I did, Tsukishiro let out a weak noise.

"...Kou...saka..."

"Tsukishiro! Do you recognize me?!"

"Yes... I... I'm still alive, aren't I...?"

"Of course you are! You didn't turn into a zombie!"

Tsukishiro appeared human, unlike when I had transformed, and the bite mark was still there. It looked like my saliva had saved her...

"...Tsukishiro, I have to go and make sure there aren't any zombies still in the dorm. I'm afraid to leave you here, though, so I'm going to carry you on my back, if you don't mind."

"That's...fine...," she said weakly. It seemed Tsukishiro still wasn't feeling all that great. I lifted her onto my back and began making my way through the dorm building.

I checked all the floors and didn't see any more zombies. Considering all the noise we'd been making in the yard, maybe they'd never made it past the second floor. Still, with just the light of my phone to go by, I couldn't say for sure that it was completely safe, so we'd have to stay on our guard until the morning.

I returned to the first floor to lay Tsukishiro on a bed, then went up to where Lisa and Ichinose were. Although the two of them looked worried, they said they hadn't sensed any zombies approaching the room. Still, considering what had happened to Tsukishiro, I asked them to stay in their rooms until morning.

I quickly returned to where Tsukishiro was on the first floor but saw no signs of her turning into a zombie. It must have been half an hour by then since she'd regained consciousness. Was it safe to assume that she was okay...?

"Tsukishiro, how are you feeling...?" I asked quietly, and she sat upright on the bed.

"It hurts where I was bitten, but I think the rest of me is fine."

"Good..."

"Thank you, Kousaka. It must have been hard for you to walk around carrying me on your back..."

"It was no big deal... Anyway, now that the threat's over, I'd like to talk to you about where we go from here."

"—What?!"

Tsukishiro looked away, her face full of embarrassment for some reason.

"...Are you saying you wish for us to be in a relationship?"

"That's not what I'm saying at all. I'm talking about whether we should tell the others that you were bitten by a zombie and managed to overcome the virus by kissing me."

"Don't say it in such a confusing way!" Tsukishiro berated me, red in the face. "Where *we're* going from here? Of course that's where my mind would go!"

"S-sorry..."

Come to think of it, Haruka gave me a similar sort of warning before...

"...I'm sorry; I guess I was a little agitated," Tsukishiro said. "...It's probably because of that long, passionate kiss from earlier, but that was all I could think about..."

"I—I see..."

"I only confessed my feelings for you because I thought I was going to die, but then you went ahead and saved me. You'll have to take responsibility for that."

"Oh, uh..."

"Hee-hee! I'm only joking, of course. I'm grateful to you for saving my life, Kousaka, and I couldn't ask for anything more. So back to the topic at hand; what we need to decide now is whether to tell everyone about what just happened, right?"

"Right. I think it would only worry them finding out that two of their dorm mates have been bitten by zombies—"

"I think we should tell them," Tsukishiro said firmly. "I'll leave it to you to decide if you want to tell them about yourself, Kousaka. However, I think the right thing to do is to tell them everything and let them decide whether we can stay in this dorm."

"What if they kick us out, though?!"

"I'll accept their decision and look for another place to use as a base."

"……"

Tsukishiro was right about everything.

That said, it was one thing to be *right* and another thing entirely as to whether that would help everyone.

Unlike me, Tsukishiro couldn't turn herself into a zombie whenever she wanted. I couldn't imagine that she would survive if she left the dorm, but maybe that was a risk she was willing to take…

"Kousaka? Is something wrong?"

"It's nothing. Okay then, we'll tell everyone about us tomorrow."

"Thank you." Tsukishiro bowed deeply to me, a determined look on her face. "…Also, I was on duty guarding the gate tonight, so do you think I should I go back?"

"No, I'm worried about your condition, so rest up for tonight. I'll take your place on guard duty. Come and tell me right away if you start to feel strange."

"I will. Thank you."

As soon as she said that, Tsukishiro went to lie down on the bed. She'd probably only been putting up a strong front and still wasn't feeling all that well… It wasn't as if I could do anything by being here, though, as I'd only get in the way of her rest. I silently went out to the yard and got into the passenger seat of the car. Haruka was still in the driver's seat—and she immediately began complaining.

"You said you were bringing Tsukishiro and that other woman to the car. What have you been doing for over an hour?"

"Oh, sorry... A lot happened."

"What d'you mean?"

"......"

She was sure to get in a bad mood if I told her I'd kissed Tsukishiro. Even if I explained it was practically mouth-to-mouth resuscitation, I had a feeling Haruka wouldn't accept it. So I decided to put it off until later.

"I'll tell everyone tomorrow morning."

"What is it? Don't leave me hanging. No way... Did someone get bitten by a zombie...?"

...Her instincts were as sharp as usual.

"Actually, the woman who came here looking for help had been bitten by a zombie. So that became an issue."

"She had...?" Haruka closed her eyes and quietly put her hands together. I said a silent prayer with her.

"...I'm going to take over guard duty tonight, so you head back to the room," I told her. "Thanks for all your help."

"No, let me stay here with you... After everything that's happened, I doubt I'd be able to get any sleep anyway."

"Oh..."

We sat like that for a little while, until Haruka broke the silence with a quiet murmur.

"...I killed a lot of zombies."

"You took action. And that was the thing that helped me make up my mind to fight."

"Did I do the right thing, though? Those zombies may have learned to communicate like you can..."

"All of us here would be dead if we hadn't killed those zombies.

Right now, that's all that matters… Still, I don't want to kill any more zombies, either, if we can help it. I think we need to come up with a system for the base so we won't have to fight them. Maybe we could set up a second gate so zombies can't get in right away, even if they breach one of them. We could also build a deep moat around the fence so zombies can't get near us."

"That's brilliant…! You sure are good at coming up with ideas, Yuuma…!"

"Still, it wouldn't be enough to deal with that three-meter-plus zombie. Something like that would probably be able to easily climb over a moat and the fence…"

"What was the deal with that huge zombie?"

"No idea, it must have mutated or something; I'm pretty sure the tallest person in the world is around two hundred and seventy centimeters. Maybe something weird happened when the zombie virus entered their body, different than how it affected me… I can't picture us being able to restrain a monster like that, so we'll need to have weapons ready for the next time a zombie that big shows up…"

There were a lot of other things we had to go over as well, like how to contact each other in an emergency and how to quarantine survivors who came to us seeking help for a while.

I stared at the cracked windshield, the cogs in my mind turning.

# DAY 4

The long night was finally over.

As the sky lightened, I was once again reminded of the horrific events we'd just been through. The windows of the dorm building were broken, and headless zombies were lying everywhere on the grounds.

As Haruka turned off the engine and we opened the car doors, an awful stench of decay hit me.

"…I want to bury these people as soon as possible," she said. "I feel bad leaving them just lying around…"

"Yeah. We'll dig a hole somewhere and bury them. I think I saw a shovel in the shed."

"I'd like to mourn them and plant flowers where we bury them…"

"You have a kind heart, Haruka. We'll bring them some flowers later."

So just like that, we decided to bury the zombies we'd killed.

After returning to my room and getting changed, I went out into the yard to dig the huge hole. As soon as I started digging, Tsukishiro came out, hearing the noise.

"Kousaka. Thank you for taking over my watch last night."

"No problem. Did you get some rest?"

"A bit... I couldn't sleep at all, but I feel much better after lying there with my eyes closed."

"I'm glad to hear that. You almost died last night, so it's no wonder that you couldn't sleep."

Tsukishiro blushed, hearing me console her.

"...The main reason I couldn't sleep was because the person I have a crush on kissed me," Tsukishiro said, so softly that only I could hear. There was a hint of reproach in her voice.

Lisa and Ichinose eventually joined us in the yard, and all five of us began to bury the bodies. We carried the headless zombies into the hole, being careful not to get any of their bodily fluids on us.

By the time we finished burying the last zombie, more than two hours had passed. I filled in the hole, and we turned to the grave and said a silent prayer.

Tsukishiro was standing next to me, and it was at that point that I noticed something strange was going on with her. Her breathing was labored, and just standing there seemed to be a challenge.

"Tsukishiro...? Are you all right...?"

She crumpled to the ground, and when I touched her hand, it was surprisingly cold.

Had the zombification started happening again...?!

"Kousaka... It hurts...!! Kiss me again—"

I cut Tsukishiro off, pressing my mouth against hers and began giving her my saliva.

Haruka and the others were stunned, but there was no time to explain.

"...Mmm...! ...Aaahh...!"

Our breathing came heavy as we continued to kiss deeply.

After a while, her hand started to warm up. I decided to stop kissing Tsukishiro and see how she was doing.

It was only then that my eyes met Haruka's. She was glaring at me with a horrified look on her face. Her fists were clenched, and her body shook in anger.

"H...hey, what are you doing, cheating on me in broad daylight?!"

"No, you don't understand..."

I looked around as I tried to plead my case, but Ichinose looked away in embarrassment, and Lisa stared at me in disbelief. They all had completely the wrong idea—not that I could blame them, though. The way they saw it, Tsukishiro and I were an obscene couple who had suddenly started to make out in front of everyone.

I had everyone move to the cafeteria, where I told them everything. I explained that I could turn into a zombie without losing my consciousness as a human and recounted Tsukishiro being bitten the night before.

"—So that's the whole story. It doesn't look like the zombie virus in Tsukishiro's body has died yet, though. Maybe it recovers when the bacteria from my saliva decreases."

"So, Yuuma, you're saying you have to kiss Tsukishiro every time she starts turning into a zombie...? And not only that, but you have to *French kiss* each time, because you have to feed her your saliva...?" said a shocked Haruka.

"Pretty much..."

"It's incredibly painful when the zombie virus activates, so, Kousaka, I want you to kiss me regularly so the bacteria in my body doesn't drop below a certain amount…"

"Yeah, that makes sense. The pain flared up again about seven hours after we kissed last night, so one kiss every six hours is probably best."

Haruka's eyes widened. "You're going to kiss her like that *four times a day*…?!"

Tsukishiro shirked back, feeling responsible for the situation we'd found ourselves in.

"I'm sorry, Kousaka. This is all my fault…"

"Don't worry about it. You wouldn't have been bitten in the first place if I'd told you I was a zombie sooner."

"But I'm sure you don't feel comfortable kissing me in front of everyone all the time…"

"It's more like mouth-to-mouth resuscitation, so I don't think the others mind."

"No, Yuuma, we *do* mind," interjected Haruka.

"You do? Then I'll make sure Tsukishiro and I are alone when we kiss."

"Ngh…! I don't like that, either…"

"Which is it?"

"I don't want to watch the two of you kissing in front of me, but if you do it where I can't see you, I'll end up imagining you getting carried away."

"We won't get carried away. I have the zombie virus in my body, and—"

It was at that moment I realized something crucial.

As long as it was with Tsukishiro, I could have sex.

\* \* \*

In fact, having the zombie virus in our bodies made it impossible for either of us to do it with anyone else. And on top of that, Tsukishiro had feelings for me…

"……"

I could feel the silent stares of the four girls focused on me. Were they looking at me suspiciously because I'd stopped talking mid-sentence to entertain my sexual fantasies?

"…Let's get back on track. Kissing once every six hours means we'll have to be together almost all the time. You'd have to come with me when I go out to get food, sleep in the same room as me, and we'd have to kiss before going to bed and right after we wake up—"

"What are you, a couple who's just moved in together?!" Haruka complained. But I ignored her, since this was how it had to be.

"For the time being, I think Tsukishiro and I should use a room on the ground floor."

"I'm sleeping in the same room!" yelled Haruka. "No arguments!"

"We don't have enough beds, though."

"I'll bring one in from another room! There'll be plenty of space if we remove the rest of the furniture!"

"I guess that's…not impossible…"

"I think I'll sleep in your room, too, then," Lisa said. "We should all be together if something happens like it did last night. It's really scary being in a room by yourself."

"…I'd also like to join you, if you don't mind," added Ichinose.

They had a point; it was definitely more convenient from a security standpoint for all five of us to sleep in the same room.

"Considering how wide they are, one room should be able to fit three bunk beds, as long as we put our belongings somewhere else."

And just like that it was decided: Everyone would move in together.

After a quick breakfast, we rearranged the furniture. It didn't take that long in the end, since all five of us pitched in to disassemble the bunk beds and move things around.

Once we were done, Haruka and I decided to go out to the supermarket to pick up flashlights and other supplies we'd need at night. Of course Tsukishiro would have to come with us.

There was a big crack in the front window of Haruka's car from last night's battle, so we'd need another one. The small pickup truck was still in one piece, but it was a two-seater...

Before heading out, I caught Haruka in the hallway of the dorm to go over the plan.

"I'll drive the pickup to the same supermarket as before. What're you gonna do?"

"You're letting Tsukishiro sit in the passenger seat, right?"

"Well, yeah."

"Tsukishiro—and *not* your girlfriend."

"Don't sulk."

"I'll drive my car and follow you."

"Are you sure? The windshield's cracked."

"With my driving skills, it won't be a problem."

"You're so reliable. Thanks, that's a big help."

"Don't worry about it. Well, then, I guess I'll enjoy my car ride all alone..."

"...Don't let Tsukishiro hear you talking sarcastically like that."

"I won't. I only say things like that when we're alone," Haruka said, glaring at me. Apparently, she still wasn't happy about the situation between Tsukishiro and me.

With the three of us split up into two vehicles, Haruka, Tsukishiro, and I arrived at the parking lot of the supermarket. Our first order of business was to get a new vehicle.

Using the car keys I found on the zombies lying in the stockroom, we went around starting the cars in the lot. I eventually found a blue sedan that had almost a full tank of gasoline and decided to take it.

The automatic door had stopped working due to the power outage, so I pried it open, and the girls and I went into the store looking for battery-powered lights. Walking around, we found flashlights and electric lanterns, as well as several types of motion-sensor lights. Nighttime guard duty should be a little easier if we attached these to the gate.

I was packing the assortment of lights into the car when I noticed Tsukishiro looking down at the ground in embarrassment.

"Tsukishiro…?"

"…Sorry. It's been almost six hours, so…"

"Oh…! Right…"

"But…it's embarrassing to do it out here, so I was hoping we could do it in the car…"

"Sure thing."

We got into the sedan I'd just picked up and closed the doors. I leaned over from the driver's seat to kiss Tsukishiro, who was sitting in the passenger seat. Haruka stood outside glaring at us as I began to give Tsukishiro my saliva.

As I did, Tsukishiro's tongue, which she'd hardly moved when we'd kissed before, worked its way between my teeth and began invading deeper into my mouth. It squirmed around and sucked up the saliva.

...Shit. She was getting me excited.

Even though I kept telling myself that this was nothing more than a medical procedure, I couldn't stop my body temperature from rising. The guilty pleasure was intoxicating, but somehow, I managed to stay rational. I ended the kiss after about three minutes. Our lips parted, and we stepped out of the car breathing heavily.

Once we were back in the supermarket, we picked up portable stoves and gas canisters, then went to the frozen food section, took items that were beginning to thaw out, and carried everything back to the car.

That was the end of our grocery shopping for the day. We returned to the dorm, and after I finished eating lunch, I went around the building installing our new lights.

When it got a bit later in the afternoon, we headed out to the riverbank for a drum bath. We brought five portable stoves and gas canisters, so we figured we'd be able to make more hot water than we had the day before. As we waited for the water to heat up, we all changed into our swimsuits, and I noticed that another six hours had passed since our last kiss.

Tsukishiro and I were pressed together in our swimsuits, and we gazed out at the sunset as we kissed. It was tough to keep my lower body from reacting to the feel of her breasts on my body.

That night, we'd all moved into the new bedroom, and Tsukishiro and I were about to kiss before going to bed. Figuring it'd be easier to give her my saliva with the help of gravity, I had Tsukishiro lie on her back as I kissed her.

As soon as I finished kissing her, I heard a scream.

"—Aaahh!! I can't take this anymore!!" Haruka shouted. "You've been kissing her all day long!! In the car, on the riverbank as the sun

set, in bed!! You've been kissing her in all sorts of different settings!!
I'm jealous!!"

Haruka suddenly closed the distance between us, and glaring
at me, she made an outrageous demand.

"Yuuma!! I want you to kiss me, too!!"

"You know I can't do that."

"Sure, you can! It's okay, as long as I don't get your saliva in my
mouth!"

"What if I give you the zombie virus?"

"If it takes turning into a zombie to kiss you, then I accept!"

"Don't say something so ridiculous…"

Although I was dumbfounded, it seemed dangerous to ignore
Haruka's feelings any longer, so the two of us left the bedroom and
went up to the rooftop where we wouldn't have to worry about the
others.

"…Haruka. Do you really want to kiss me that badly?"

"—Yeah, I do," she said with a look of determination.

"…Okay, then. I'll kiss you."

"—! You will?"

"Yeah. But just remember, you'll be kicked out of here if you turn
into a zombie and lose your mind."

"I'm aware of that."

"Good. Oh, and just so you know…even if you're kicked out, I'll
keep on kissing Tsukishiro every day."

Even though I was only stating the obvious, Haruka scowled
at me.

"Also, Tsukishiro told me she likes me yesterday."

"What?!"

"I didn't reply to her, seeing as I have a girlfriend now, but if you turn into a zombie and disappear...you know."

"N-no way!! You should mourn me until the day you die!!"

"I can't do that. Besides, Tsukishiro is the only person I can have sex with."

"Ngh... Hngh...!!"

"Okay then, you ready?"

I took a step closer, but Haruka covered her lips with her hands.

"Yuuma, that's not fair. You know I'd do whatever it took to stop you if you said you might get together with Tsukishiro."

"So now you *do* care if you become a zombie?"

"Not only that, I'll even drink muddy water if I have to—just to survive. I will never allow you to live happily ever after with anyone besides me."

Her purpose in life was so backward it was scary.

"Relax, Haruka. I'll make sure you never have to drink muddy water... I'll protect you, forever."

"—Huh?! Forever?!"

"Yeah, I have to, since the world's full of zombies."

"Yeah, but...forever, huh...? Hee-hee-hee."

A dumb smile crossed Haruka's face. I guess her mood had improved.

"Okay. I'll be counting on you, then. But...I have one request. You kissing Tsukishiro is like torture to me, so I want you to find a way for her to stay human without kissing her."

"You're asking me to find a way to kill the zombie virus inside her?"

"That's right. Let's figure out what exactly it is that's turning people into zombies and create a vaccine."

"That's a pretty high bar..."

"Then I'll make it an order instead of a request. Find a way for Tsukishiro to stay human without kissing her," Haruka demanded with a glare.

I'm the strongest in this zombie world, but I can't beat this girl.

# DAY 5

I was woken up before dawn the next day, feeling someone slip into my bed.

"…Excuse me, Kousaka. It's almost four o'clock…"

It was Tsukishiro. I'd kissed her at ten last night when we'd gone to bed, so she had to refuel before morning.

I was about to sit up, but she pushed me back down.

"…I'd like to be on top this time."

"—Huh?"

"Hee-hee! I was thinking we might as well try different positions while we're at it."

The next moment, Tsukishiro leaned in and stole my lips. Her tongue entered through the gap in my teeth and sucked up the saliva in my mouth.

*Shit. The lower half of my body's starting to react—*

"…Kousaka. I feel something hard pressing against me…"

Tsukishiro had pulled her lips away from mine and turned her gaze downward.

"S-sorry…!!"

"Are you getting aroused kissing me, by any chance?" Tsukishiro whispered in my ear as she put her arms around me. "...Kousaka. I overheard you and Hyuuga talking last night."

"You did...?"

"You said I was the only person you could have sex with."

"—!! That was just to convince Haruka—"

"But what you said is true, isn't it?"

"Well, uh..."

"If you want to..." Tsukishiro trailed off and put her forehead against my chest. "...So? What do you say?"

"Wh-what d'you mean...?"

This was way too unexpected. I'd never imagined that Tsukishiro would say something like that...

Apparently, Haruka wasn't the only girl I was powerless against.

# AFTERWORD

For five years now, I've wanted to write a romcom with zombies as the subject, but I'd given up on the idea after often hearing that light novels about zombies didn't sell.

But last year, I couldn't take it anymore and sent in a proposal on a whim, so I was surprised when it got picked up without a hitch. Perhaps it was because my previous work, *The Girl Who Came In First Place at the Best Potential Bride Contest Has Me Under Her Thumb*, had been very well received. As I always thought, girls who have you under their thumb are the right way to go.

Hi, everyone, I'm Ryou Iwanami, the author of this book. I started working at a gaming company last year because I really wanted to work with younger women. It turned out to be hopeless, though, because the job is completely remote, so I have no opportunities whatsoever to interact with my colleagues.

To brighten up my day, TwinBox drew these beautiful illustrations for me. Both the color pictures and black-and-white ones are all perfect, and I give thanks for them each and every day. I'm so glad to be alive…!!

Finally, I would like to extend my utmost gratitude to all the people reading this. Thank you all so much.

Since I'm a guy who loves googling myself, it would be great if you could offer positive feedback on Twitter and other sites. Negative feedback depresses me, so I'd really appreciate it if you could keep that to yourself... It would also be a great help if you could also include the book title, *I'm the Strongest in This Zombie World, but I Can't Beat This Girl!* in your comments, because it makes them easier to find.

Whether we can publish the second volume depends on the sales of the first, so I'm wishing with everything I have that I'll be able to see you all again!!

*Ryou Iwanami*
*December 2022*